A Dangerous Reputation

✪ ✪ ✪

"What do you want?" Sheriff Carpenter's voice came from deep in his chest, and he showed teeth that were brown from too much coffee and too many cigaritos.

From his shirt Sam drew a worn, sweat-stained paper. He unfolded it and tossed it on Carpenter's desk.

"It's a reward notice for somebody named Cole Chandler. So what?"

Sam jerked a thumb toward the door. "Cole's outside. Under the blanket."

Sheriff Carpenter glanced over Sam's shoulder, out the door.

"I've come to claim the reward," Sam went on.

Carpenter snorted. "Bounty hunter, huh? You'll have to wait. I've got a posse to lead. I don't have time to telegraph"—he read the reward notice again—"Lordsburg for the authority to get you paid. The bank's just been robbed, so there's no money to pay you, anyway, Mister . . . ?"

"Slater. Sam Slater."

Carpenter stood straighter. He seemed to notice Sam for the first time. "The Regulator?"

Also by Dale Colter

The Regulator
Diablo at Daybreak
Deadly Justice
Dead Man's Ride
Gravedancer
The Scalp Hunters
Paradise Mountain

Published by
HARPERPAPERBACKS

DALE COLTER

THE REGULATOR

DESERT PURSUIT

HarperPaperbacks
A Division of HarperCollins*Publishers*

HarperPaperbacks *A Division of* HarperCollins*Publishers*
10 East 53rd Street, New York, N.Y. 10022

Cover illustration by Miro

First printing: November 1992

Printed in the United States of America

HarperPaperbacks and colophon are trademarks of HarperCollins*Publishers*

❖ 10 9 8 7 6 5 4 3 2 1

THE CLOCK ON THE WALL OF SAN MIGUEL'S only bank read 9:23, but no one was paying attention. The bank's two tellers and a pair of early-morning customers were staring down the barrels of pistols being held on them by a gang of masked men. The bank's third employee, the manager, fumbled nervously with the safe's combination lock.

There were six bandits. They had entered the bank in groups of three. Suddenly their leader and two others had drawn pistols, vaulted the tellers' counter, and covered the employees. Two more bandits had drawn down on the customers while a third had watched the front door.

"Hurry up with that safe!" barked the bandit leader. He was a tall, rangy fellow named Gus Grissom, though the bandits were careful not to call one another by name in front of witnesses.

Murdoch, the bank manager, wiped his sweaty hands down the front of his suit coat and tried again. In his fright his pudgy fingers seemed incapable of lining up the lock's correct numbers.

Another bandit, a skinny blond named Virge Harper, stepped close to the manager. "Hurry up, damn you, or I'll blow your brains all over this room."

"Easy, *compadre*," said the third man behind the counter. He was a Mexican called Paco, and he wore the garb of a vaquero, which he had once been. "Kill him, and we will never get the money."

Virge saw the truth in that statement, and he stepped back, though reluctantly. As he did so Murdoch finally got the combination right. The tumblers fell into place. Breathing easier, Murdoch pulled down the lever and hauled open the safe's heavy iron door, revealing bags of coins and bound stacks of greenbacks.

The bandits looked at their haul, wide-eyed. "You were right, amigo," Gus said, congratulating Paco. "This place is a goddamn gold mine."

Gus pulled two empty grain sacks from under his shirt. He tossed one to Virge, and the two men knelt, sweeping money out of the safe and into the sacks.

In the front room the two customers stood with their hands raised nervously. One was a grocer, come to make a withdrawal so that he would have cash on hand for the day's business. The other was a young teamster, saving so that he could marry his girl and make a down payment on a small freight outfit of his own. They were covered by a big, mean-looking breed called Cherokee Bill and an ex-Confederate cavalryman called Little Tom. Joe Crist, the youngest of the bandits, peered from behind the dark curtain that hung as a sunscreen across the door's windows.

"Anybody coming?" Little Tom asked Joe.

"Not yet," Joe answered. He licked his lips. "Street's filling up, though. Bound to be somebody here soon."

"We are almost done in here," Paco reassured them from behind the counter.

At that moment one of the tellers decided to be a hero.

He was a nineteen-year-old named Barry, and he must have thought he was indestructible. As Paco glanced across the counter at his friends, Barry, who had been waiting for such a chance, leaped on the Mexican, grabbing for his gun. The two men crashed to the floor. Barry yanked the pistol from the surprised Paco's hand. Barry whirled, but before he could do anything else, Gus Grissom snatched his own pistol from the floor and shot the young teller twice at close quarters.

Barry cried out and fell forward, bouncing against Gus, knocking the bandanna loose from the outlaw's sweaty face.

"Christ," swore Joe, looking out the front door. "You just alerted the whole town."

Gus didn't hear. Mask down, he was staring at Murdoch. The bank manager was looking at him as well, obviously memorizing Gus's dark, handsome features.

For a heartbeat the room was quiet. A wreath of powder smoke hung heavy in the morning heat. Then Gus put his pistol to Murdoch's forehead and pulled the trigger. The bank manager was slammed back against the open door of the safe. He dropped to the floor, leaving a smear of blood and gray material on the iron door.

"What did you do that for?" said Paco, who had risen to his feet.

"He saw my face," Gus told him. "I don't want to be identified. You don't want me to be identified, either. Kill 'em all."

That was the kind of order Virge liked. Chuckling beneath his bandanna, the skinny blond shot the other teller twice in the chest. He was so close to the man that the teller's starched shirt caught fire from the muzzle flashes. In the front room the young teamster turned and tried to run, but he was cut down by Cherokee Bill.

The grocer fell to his knees, pleading. "No! No! I won't tell. I swear it. Please, I have a wife and—"

A shot from Little Tom's pistol ended his speech. The grocer toppled onto his side with the top of his head blown apart.

"Oh God," moaned Joe, looking at the carnage. He wished he had never joined this bunch.

Gus turned back to the safe. "Hurry up with this money!"

While Paco stamped out the fire on the dead teller's chest, Gus and Virge stuffed the rest of the money into the grain sacks. Virge dropped a bag full of five-dollar gold pieces. The bag broke open and coins spilled all over the floor. Virge tried to pick them up. "Leave them," Gus told him. "There's no time."

"Hurry," Joe urged from the front. "There's people gathering, and they've got guns."

Gus threw the last bundle of bills into the grain sack. "Come on!" he said.

Gus, Virge, and Paco went back over the counter. Slipping in the blood on the floor, the six bandits dashed out the front door. They ran to their horses, which were plunging and neighing with excitement from the gunfire. Gus and Virge looped the grain sacks across their saddle pommels. The bandits unhitched their horses and mounted. Across the street the armed townspeople were taking cover. Rifle and pistol shots were directed at the bandits, who replied in kind.

"Let's ride!" Gus said.

The six bandits thundered down San Miguel's main street, with guns blazing at them from all sides. At the street's far end they found their way blocked by a barricade of wagons and buckboards, manhandled into place by the resourceful townsmen. There was a volley of gunfire from behind the barricade. Young Joe Crist reeled in the saddle, clutching his shoulder. Paco's horse stumbled, blood pumping from its neck.

The bandits reined in. Their horses stamped and pawed the air in a cloud of dust. "Come on," Gus cried. "The other way."

The bandits wheeled and galloped back down the street, running a gauntlet of fire. Little Tom was hit. He fell from the saddle and bounced hard. He staggered to his feet, crying, "Gus!" But Gus and the others did not come back for him. Holding his wounded side, Tom picked up his pistol from the street. At that moment the townsmen, who had been watching him, opened up. One bullet spun Tom around. Another dropped him to one knee. Tom raised his own weapon and tried to fire, but bullet after bullet pulped into his body, making him shudder, until at last he fell forward on his face and did not move.

The remaining bandits continued their dash for safety, firing back at their tormentors. When their pistols were empty, they holstered them and drew fresh ones from their belts.

At the far end of the street another group of townsmen was trying to repeat the success of its neighbors, pushing a pair of big Murphy wagons together to block the street. "Keep going!" Gus cried. "We can't turn back!"

There was only a small gap between the wagons, where the tongues overlapped. Gus fired at the laboring townsmen, dropping one. He spurred his horse forward, eyes fixed on the narrowing gap. He galloped up and jumped his mount over the wagon tongues. The other bandits followed his example, first Virge, then Cherokee Bill. The wounded Joe Crist came next. As his horse finished the jump Joe slipped and almost fell from the saddle. Bringing up the rear, Paco reached over and steadied him, and the two of them kept going.

Whooping with exhilaration at having survived, the bandits rode out of San Miguel. They passed a stagecoach that had pulled over to the side of the street for safety, and they threw lead its way for the sheer hell of it. While the stage driver struggled to curb his rearing team, a well-dressed woman with reddish hair leaned from the coach window. As the woman watched the bandits disappear in a long plume of dust, she swore a most unladylike oath.

The bandits galloped along the flats outside town, putting distance between themselves and the inevitable pursuit. Two of the horses—Paco's and Virge's—had been hit. Neither was bad yet, but they would never make Mexico, which was the gang's destination.

"How you doing, kid?" Gus yelled back to Joe Crist.

Slumped in his saddle, Joe looked up with pain on his youthful face. "I'm all right."

About a mile from town the bandits spotted a rider headed their way. The rider was tall, and he led a horse across whose back was slung a blanket-covered bundle.

"There's two new horses for us," Virge said, and the bandits swung their mounts in the rider's direction.

The tall rider, who knew trouble when he saw it coming, drew his saddle gun, aimed, and sent a bullet over the advancing bandits' heads.

Gus reined in. "That was too close for me, boys. This hombre's like to prove more trouble than he's worth. His animals look done in, anyway. Come on, we'll find fresh mounts somewhere else."

The bandits gave the tall rider a wide berth, and they continued down the road.

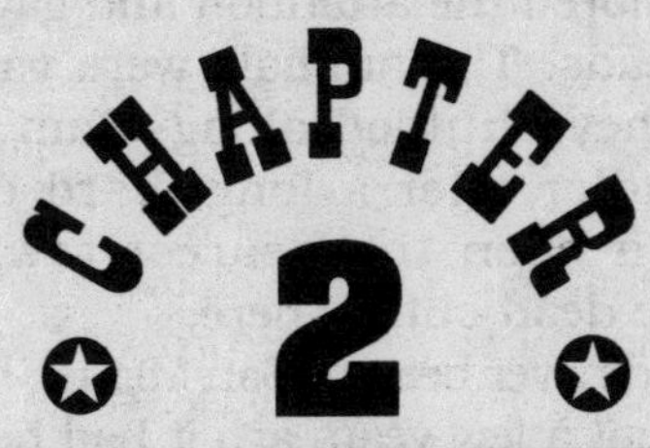

THE TALL RIDER ENTERED SAN MIGUEL leading a horse with the blanket-wrapped body of Cole Chandler tied across its back.

Cole Chandler was—or had been—a horse thief and small-time gunman. Now he was rotting beneath his own threadbare blanket. The smell was so bad that it turned heads even in the crowded, excited main street of San Miguel.

Men stared at the ripe bundle. They stared at the tall rider who had brought it in—unshaven, dirty, saddle weary. The rider had a crooked nose and a scar that ran from his left ear to the corner of his mouth.

"Jesus, that's Sam Slater," someone said.

"It's the Regulator."

Sam ignored the attention and gave his horses their heads. The animals were gaunt, heads down as they shuffled along. Sam had taken Cole Chandler after a long, hard chase. San Miguel had been the nearest town, so he'd brought the dead outlaw here.

Sam had never been to San Miguel, but he knew about it. Until a few years ago it had been a sleepy water hole inhabited mainly by Mexicans. Now it was a bustling town of adobe and tents, its prosperity fueled by nearby copper mines and ranches.

The town's growth had not been matched by a corresponding cleanliness. The streets were full of manure and garbage. There was even a dead mule at one intersection, around which men guided animals and vehicles. The town must be waiting for jailhouse labor to remove the remains. A terrific stench filled the air, both from the many privies and from the flats east of town, where cattle were slaughtered for food and their carcasses left to rot.

Sam passed the bullet-riddled body of a man propped on a board. Grinning men with rifles were taking turns having their photographs taken with the body. Sam remembered his run-in with the five riders outside town. He figured they were somehow connected with what was left of this fellow.

"What happened here?" he asked a prosperous-looking young man who had just been photographed with the corpse.

"Holdup," replied the man. "There was six of

'em. They cleaned out the bank, killed six men altogether. Sheriff Carpenter's getting together a posse to go after the rest."

The man's companion grabbed him by the arm. "Come on, Tony, you going?"

"I sure am," said Tony. "I had over five hundred dollars in that bank. If I don't get it back, my business will be wiped out. My wife and I will lose that new home we had built."

"Get dressed, then. We got to get some horses."

Tony and his companion hurried down the street. Sam found the sheriff's office and stopped in front of it. He dismounted, hitched his weary horses to the rail, and stepped up under the awning shade. His knee-high Apache moccasins made no sound on the sidewalk boards. The office door was open, and Sam went in.

Sheriff Carpenter and his deputy were loading rifles, shotguns, pistols. They stuffed spare shells and shirts into their saddlebags.

"Ed, go see what's taking Mabry so long with those horses," said the sheriff. He was a rock-jawed fellow of medium height, with a dark mustache and hair just starting to thin.

"Right," said the young deputy. He threw a wary glance at the scarred stranger and sidled past him, out the door.

"What do you want?" Sheriff Carpenter's voice came from deep in his chest, and he showed teeth that were brown from too much coffee and too many cigaritos.

From his shirt Sam drew a worn, sweat-stained paper. He unfolded it and tossed it on Carpenter's desk.

"It's a reward notice for somebody named Cole Chandler. So what?"

Sam jerked a thumb toward the door. "Cole's outside. Under the blanket."

Sheriff Carpenter glanced over Sam's shoulder, out the door.

"I've come to claim the reward," Sam went on.

Carpenter snorted. "Bounty hunter, huh? You'll have to wait. I've got a posse to lead. I don't have time to telegraph"—he read the reward notice again—"Lordsburg for the authority to get you paid. The bank's just been robbed, so there's no money to pay you, anyway, Mister . . . ?"

"Slater. Sam Slater."

Carpenter stood straighter. He seemed to notice Sam for the first time. "The Regulator?"

"I've been called that."

The sheriff eyed the scarred, dusty stranger. "I've heard about you, Slater. They say you can track a fly through shit and you're impossible to kill. You know, you'd be just the fellow we need to help us catch these bank robbers. Posse's leaving in a few minutes. I realize you're all in, but having you along would help us a lot. What do you say?"

Sam furrowed his brow. "You know who they were?"

Carpenter shook his head. "Nobody saw their faces—nobody that lived. They killed six men—five in the bank and one in the shoot-out afterward, plus another three wounded. They weren't local boys, though, I'd stake my retirement on that—if I had any."

"The bank putting up a reward?"

"We don't need a reward for bringing back our own money and catching the bastard that killed our friends. We're doing this out of civic duty."

Sam said, "In that case I think I'll sit this one out."

Carpenter looked surprised. "Don't you care what these men did? Don't you want to see them brought to justice?"

Sam didn't rise to the bait. "Sure I do, Sheriff, but chasing bad men is my work, and I don't work for free."

"I'm disappointed in you, Slater. Disappointed that you seem to equate justice with making money."

"I don't see you giving up your salary," Sam pointed out.

"I have to make a living."

"So do I."

"Have it your way, then," Carpenter grumbled. "But if you want your money, you'll have to wait for it."

"Fine by me," Sam said. "In the meantime what do I do with Chandler's body?"

"That's your problem."

Carpenter clapped on his hat. He picked up his saddlebags and shotgun and started for the street. "Close the door behind you when you leave," he told Sam.

Sam grinned and followed the sheriff outside,

where the posse was forming. The young deputy called Ed had brought up a saddled black horse, upon which Sheriff Carpenter tied his saddlebags. He thrust the shotgun into a pommel scabbard.

There were a dozen men in the posse, along with three extra horses carrying supplies and water bags. The men looked fit and well armed, and they knew who Sam was. "Is Mr. Slater going with us?" the prosperous-looking young man named Tony asked hopefully.

"No!" said Carpenter.

"Which way was them robbers headed?" asked another man, a heavyset miner, who had just ridden up.

"Southeast," replied the deputy, Ed. "Into the desert."

The novice lawman whistled. "Water's scarce in them parts."

"No shit," said Sheriff Carpenter as he retightened the horse's saddle girths. "It's scarce around here, too, in case you hadn't noticed. Don't go if you don't want to."

Another posse member, a clean-shaven fellow with the cool look of a gunman, said, "What about Apaches? Is Chiquito still on the warpath?"

Carpenter mounted. "There's been no Injun sign for two weeks. Wherever Chiquito's at, it's not around here."

Sam frowned. He had heard of Chiquito, though he'd never met him during his years as an adopted captive of the Apaches. Chiquito was a war chief of the Mimbres Apaches, considered the most cunning of the Apache bands.

Carpenter settled himself firmly in the saddle, and his deep voice boomed. "Now, has anybody else got something they'd like to know—like what day does Christmas come on this year, or what does President Grant take for his hangovers?"

No one did.

"All right. Let's go catch some bank robbers."

With a dirty look at Sam the sheriff jerked his horse around and started out of town, followed by the deputy, Ed, and the rest of the posse, with the packhorses bringing up the rear. As they got down the street they broke into a lope, scattering people and animals in their path. In his haste to get out of their way one man tripped over the dead mule and fell, to the amusement of the onlookers.

Sam watched them go. Then he untied Cole Chandler's stinking body from its horse. He hoisted the blanket-wrapped body onto his shoulder and carried it into the sheriff's office, where he deposited it in Sheriff Carpenter's chair.

"Wait here," he told the corpse. Then he shut the door and went back outside.

He walked the horses to the nearest stable, where he stabled his own and sold Chandler's. The stabler gave him thirty dollars for Chandler's horse. That gave Sam a total of thirty-two dollars to his name. Sometimes he wondered what he did with all the money he made.

He left the stable and started down the street. It was hot. The noontime shadows were etched sharply in the dust. He turned and entered an adobe saloon. It was dark and cool inside the saloon, black almost, after the intense brightness of the street. The floor smelled of stale sawdust.

The saloon was full of men—drinking, playing cards, and talking about the robbery. "Beer," Sam told the barkeep.

The bartender drew a mug of beer. "Two bits," he said.

"For a *beer*?" Sam had expected to pay about a nickel.

The bartender, as befitting his profession, was philosophical. "Flush times, mister. You got to pay for them."

"Somebody already has," Sam told him. "The bank's been robbed." If everything in San Miguel was as expensive as this beer, Sam's thirty-two dollars wasn't going to last long. He hoped Sheriff Carpenter came back soon.

Sam took his beer to a vacant table. He eased his weary bones into the chair, and he sipped the cooling liquid. His eyes half closed as they became accustomed to the dim light. He sighed, at peace. He could almost fall asleep here. . . .

The room suddenly became quiet.

Light footsteps sounded behind Sam's chair, and a woman's voice said, "Mr. Slater?"

SAM LOOKED UP TO SEE A WELL-DRESSED young woman whose reddish hair was worn in a shorter-than-fashionable style. She had a straight back and firm jaw, with thin, determined lips.

"Hey!" cried the barkeep. "This is a saloon. Can't you read the sign outside—women ain't allowed."

"I'm not a woman, I'm a lady. And I'll thank you to watch your tone of voice when you address me."

"Yes, ma'am," said the barkeep, taken aback. Meekly he added, "But the sign . . . ?"

"Who cares about your silly sign? Change it, if it bothers you so much."

"Yes, ma'am."

Everyone in the adobe saloon was staring at

the young woman. "Well?" she demanded, looking around at them.

They all turned away and went back to what they had been doing, but they continue to watch her discreetly from the corners of their eyes.

Sam rose from his chair. He would have preferred to have taken a nap.

The woman looked him straight in the eye. Her eyes were emerald green, exactly matching the color of her traveling dress and small, feathered hat. "Mr. Slater?" she inquired. "Samuel Slater, the bounty hunter?" She spoke with a broad New England accent.

"That's me, ma'am." She was Sam's own age or younger, but he felt like a schoolboy being called to task by a particularly demanding teacher, and he couldn't help but smile.

"Do I amuse you?" she asked.

Sam's smile disappeared. "Oh no, ma'am."

"I have a business proposition for you, Mr. Slater."

Sam pulled out a chair. "Have a seat, Mrs. . . . ?"

"Manning, Carolyn Manning. And it's 'Miss.'"

"Yes, ma'am."

Carolyn Manning sat primly, and Sam pushed her chair close to the table. "Can I get you a drink?"

"I don't indulge in spirits, sir, save an occasional glass of champagne, and I doubt they carry that here."

Sam grinned as he sat beside her. "If they do, it's probably not real." He sipped his beer. "What can I do for you, Miss Manning?"

"You know that the San Miguel Bank was robbed today, and a number of men killed?"

"Yes."

"I wish to hire you to pursue the bank robbers and bring them to justice."

Sam shook his head. "I'm a bounty hunter, Miss Manning, not a hired gun."

"Your sense of ethics is commendable. Very well, I'll make it easy on you. I will personally authorize a reward for their . . . 'demise' seems to be an appropriate word."

Sam eased back in his chair and studied her. She was good-looking in a mannish way. She was bossy, too, and he bet she was a real pain in the ass.

"What kind of reward are you talking about?"

"Two thousand dollars for the leader. Another thousand for the second in command. Five hundred for each of the others. Forty-five hundred dollars in all—plus expenses, of course."

Sam raised an eyebrow. "You have that kind of money? With you?"

"I'm not in the habit of talking to hear myself."

"I'll need proof."

She glared, unused to having her word challenged. Then she reached into her traveling jacket, and from an inside pocket she drew forth a hundred-dollar bill, handling it in such a way that no one in the saloon could see it but Sam. "There's more where that came from."

Sam believed her. He drank some more beer. "The sheriff's after those bank robbers already, with a posse. Why don't you just let them do the job?"

Carolyn Manning smiled faintly. "Be honest, Mr. Slater. Do you think Sheriff Carpenter and his posse will catch those men? And if they do catch them, do you think they'll be able to subdue them and bring them in?"

"Depends on who the men are."

"I know who they are."

Sam's eyes narrowed.

"The leader's name is Gus Grissom, and his gang is as vicious a band of cutthroats as you'll find."

Sam's mind raced. It was his job to keep up on wanted men, and the name sounded familiar. "Grissom. Isn't there a reward out for him in—"

"Texas." She finished the sentence for him. "Yes, and there's rewards on at least two of his followers as well—a former cowboy called Virgil Harper and a gorilla from the Indian Territory known as Cherokee Bill."

Sam was more interested now.

"Those rewards will be yours, along with mine, if you bring these men in," Carolyn said.

"What's your interest in Grissom?" Sam asked.

"He and his men killed my father and brother, back in Texas, in a bank robbery much like the one today. I failed to obtain justice in Texas, so I pursued them on my own, following the trail of their depredations."

"That's no Texas accent you got."

"My family is from New Hampshire originally."

"Carpetbaggers?"

"Let's say we came west in search of economic opportunity. That is the American dream, I believe?"

"How did you know Grissom and his gang were headed here?"

"I guessed—correctly, as it turns out. San Miguel was the only settlement of consequence on their route. You see, I not only know who they are, I believe I know where they're headed."

"Where's that?"

"Arispe, in Sonora. One of the gang is called Paco Lopez, and that's his hometown—or so I've been told. I caught a stage here, hoping to alert the authorities, but I was too late. So—will you accept my offer?"

Sam knew the country between San Miguel and Arispe. Water would be a problem for anyone making that journey. There were only a few ways Grissom could go. If Sam could somehow reach water before the outlaws . . .

"Mr. Slater?"

Sam nodded. "I'll go." Broke as he was, he couldn't afford not to. He sighed and finished his beer. "I was just getting comfortable here, too."

"There's one more thing. I'm coming with you."

Sam almost spat out the beer. "Oh, no. I work alone, and even if I didn't, I wouldn't work with a woman."

"That's a condition for obtaining my reward, I'm afraid. If I don't go, you don't get paid."

"Look," said Sam, "I'll find them. I'll take care of them. I'll bring back the bodies as proof, anything you want, but I won't—"

"No," she said.

"Why?"

Carolyn Manning's hard eyes came alight. She leaned forward, hands clasped on the tabletop. Her husky voice was low, but it seemed to fill the entire room. "I told you they killed my father and brother. I didn't tell you that I was there to see it. I want to watch Gus Grissom when he gets what's coming to him. I want to see the look on his face. I want him to know who's responsible."

"I can sympathize with that," Sam said. "But this is dangerous country for a woman—hell, it's dangerous for a man. And it's not just Grissom you'd have to deal with—it's lack of water, rattlers, maybe even Indians. I can't be taking some . . . some tenderfoot into a situation like that."

She eased back in the chair, exuding confidence. "I think you'll find that I can take care of myself."

Sam rubbed his eyes, out of weariness and frustration.

"Forty-five hundred dollars will buy you a lot of beer, Mr. Slater."

"I'll be honest with you, lady. You're a burr under my saddle. I don't know if I can stand five more minutes of you, much less five days or so."

She smiled. "Grit your teeth and think of the money."

"I could go after Grissom by myself, you know, and collect those Texas rewards."

"You could, but you won't. I'm paying more."

Sam drummed his fingertips on the table.

Carolyn Manning watched him patiently, like a torturer waiting for her subject to break. "All right," Sam said, letting out his breath. "It's against my better judgment, but I'll do it."

"Very good, Mr. Slater. I suggest we get cracking, then."

Get cracking? Sam thought. I'd like to crack your head. "Yeah." He wished he had time for another beer, or better yet twenty. He had a feeling he was going to need them.

The two of them rose from the table and walked out of the saloon. Everyone was staring at them. Sam saw the smug look on the bartender's face.

"Oh, shut up," Sam told him.

Outside, they walked down the crowded street, attracting a good deal of attention. Carolyn Manning was the main focus of interest. In this part of the world it was rare to see a woman of any kind, far more rare to see one who wasn't a whore. People wondered why a woman like this was keeping company with a notorious bounty hunter.

"Can you ride?" Sam asked her.

She walked easily, keeping up with Sam's long strides. "I lived in Texas for eight years. Yes, I can ride."

"We'll see if we can find you a sidesaddle."

"Please. I hate those things. They're so uncomfortable. They were obviously invented by a man, to make women feel inferior."

They spent the next several hours buying horses—Sam's was in no shape for more travel—along with supplies and camping equipment. Carolyn paid for everything.

"You'll need a weapon," Sam warned her.

"I have a pistol," she said.

She showed him the pistol. It was a Moore six-shot, "teat-cartridge" revolver, .30 caliber, a cross between a derringer and a bad joke.

Sam scoffed, looking at it. "This is a hideout gun, a surprise weapon, the kind you pull out and use to shoot somebody at close range. It won't do you any good where we're going."

He handed it back. Carolyn Manning looked crestfallen. It was the first time Sam had seen her at a loss for words, and it made him feel good.

Sam didn't think she could handle anything like a Winchester or a Sharps, so he settled on a long-barreled Colt .45 with a screw-on stock that turned it into a carbine. It was suitably light enough for a woman to handle.

The afternoon was well advanced by the time they were ready to leave. Carolyn Manning had replaced her green dress with a leather riding skirt and matching short jacket, a white blouse, and a flat-crowned, Spanish-style hat.

Sam made a last check of the saddles and the packhorse. "Grissom's got a good start on us. When I saw his bunch, it looked like they were having trouble with their horses. Looked like at least one of the men was wounded, too. Still, we're going to need a lot of luck to catch them."

"I won't slow you down, I can assure you," Carolyn said.

Right, thought Sam.

The two of them mounted. Sam took the packhorse's lead line. He looked hard at Carolyn. "You're sure you want to do this?"

She rewarded him with a stony glare.

"Tell me one thing," Sam said. "How do you know I'll really go after these men? What's to keep me from just taking you out in the desert, killing you, and stealing your money? That'd be a lot easier than swapping lead with Grissom and his boys."

Carolyn's smile was as cold as a New Hampshire January. "I've heard of you, Mr. Slater. However unsavory the rest of your reputation, you're known as an honest man."

"You sure have a backhanded way of flattering a man."

"It wasn't meant to be flattery. Honesty is a basic virtue. You should expect neither reward for it nor praise. It should come naturally."

Sam rolled his eyes. "Let's get 'cracking.'"

They rode out of town.

"GOD, IT'S HOT," SAID PAGET.

The posse members were walking their horses. Paget, a gambler by profession, pulled the black silk bandanna from his neck and wiped his forehead with it.

Sheriff Carpenter said nothing. Twenty degrees hotter wouldn't have bothered him. Carpenter was from Quebec, Canada. His name had originally been Georges Charpentier, but he had anglicized it twenty-some years earlier when he'd come to the States. The main reason he'd left home was because he couldn't stand the brutal northern weather. He loved the way the desert heat seemed to make his bones glow with warmth. Sometimes he imagined he could still feel remnants of the Canadian cold lurking in his body's nether reaches, needing to be burned out.

Carpenter rolled another cigarito as he walked. He struck a match and lit it. He was in front of the posse, along with Paget, a cattleman named Barnes, and the heavyset miner called Vickery. Carpenter's young deputy, Ed Burke, and the rest of the dozen posse members were strung out behind. No one said much; the sun seemed to have beaten them into silence.

The bandits' trail was not hard to follow. They were making no effort to conceal it. "They heading for Mexico?" Carpenter asked the leathery-faced cattleman, Barnes.

"'Pears that way," replied Barnes. He had been one of the first white men into this country and he knew it better than any of the others.

"We'll have to catch them before they cross the border," Paget said. The usually well-dressed gambler looked different in his trail clothes. He had joined the posse both for some excitement and because the act would improve his image in the eyes of a town that did not always appreciate him.

Vickery, the miner, said, "How far is the border?"

"Forty mile or so," opined Barnes, tugging at his drooping, sandy mustache.

Sheriff Carpenter blew out tobacco smoke. "They're slowing down. It doesn't take a professional scout to see that. If they don't get fresh horses, we've got 'em—that is, if we keep our heads and don't burn out our own animals." He cast a look at Vickery, who had been urging a faster pace. Vickery, who had been one of the most enthusiastic of the posse's volunteers, was now starting to worry that he might get in trouble for missing shift time at the copper mine.

To Barnes, Carpenter said, "Which way you think they'll go, Charley?"

The cattleman replied without hesitation. "Dead Horse Pass. The border's closer that way, plus there's water, if you know where to find it."

Ed Burke, the deputy, came up, along with Tony Forrest, the prosperous young hardware merchant. Tony looked at the hills around them, thick with cactus and creosote. The desert quiet was somehow made even more overwhelming by the clopping of the horses' hoofs. It was a living presence. "This country gives me the willies," Tony said. "I still wish Sam Slater had come with us."

"We don't need Slater," said Paget contemptuously. Paget believed he could handle a gun as well as anyone in the territory, a belief that was supported by numerous markers in San Miguel's boot hill.

"That's right," agreed Sheriff Carpenter. "I don't want to hear that bounty hunter's name. Slater's only interest is money. In my book that makes him no better than the men we're chasing. When we catch those murdering bastards—and we *will* catch them—we'll make short work of them. They won't be shooting down unarmed men this time. Paget, Vickery, and me all have military experience, so do some of the others. Hell, Vickery was a Regular—even if he was twenty pounds lighter then. Barnes has shot it out with cattle thieves more times than he can remember. We can handle anything those bank robbers are likely to throw at us."

Tony shivered. "It's not the bank robbers I'm worried about. It's Apaches."

"I told you, boy, Apaches ain't been in these parts for two weeks now. Some other poor souls are catching hell from Chiquito and his bunch."

Ed Burke said, "You figure we'll catch these fellows tomorrow, Sheriff?"

Carpenter nodded. "Just this side of Dead Horse Pass, if that's the way they've gone." He flicked away the remains of his cigarito. "These horses are rested enough. Let's get moving."

The posse mounted and rode on.

Some miles ahead, Gus Grissom turned in the saddle. "Holding up, kid?"

Joe Crist nodded, wincing. The Mexican, Paco, had cut up a spare shirt and made a bandage for the boy's shoulder, but the wound continued to bleed. Riding alongside Joe, Paco was worried, both about Joe and about his own wounded horse.

"Think we're being chased?" asked Virge Harper.

Gus's tone was sarcastic. "No, I think they're just going to let us take their money and ride away with it. Of course we're being chased. Like as not, you'll be able to see their dust by sundown."

"We got ourselves in a fix, and that's for certain," Virge said. The skinny ex-cowboy had a blond brush of beard beneath his loose lower lip. He looked down. His horse's right hind leg was wet with blood from a bullet it had taken in its croup, and it was beginning to limp. Virge had already transferred his heavy moneybags to Gus's mount. He tried to keep the fear of what might happen out of his voice. "If that damn fool teller hadn't screwed us, we'd've been out of that bank without a scratch."

Gus agreed with him. "Sure beats me why some people want to die for other folks' money."

"Kind of like us, huh?" joked Joe Crist.

"Not like us at all," Gus said. "I don't intend on dying."

"What about Little Tom?" countered Joe. "He didn't intend to die, neither."

"Little Tom had a bad day."

A wave of pain washed over Joe. He closed his eyes till it passed.

Paco said, "Hang on, amigo. Everything will be all right when we get to Arispe. You will see. We are just going to lie around there and take things easy. We will drink *aguardiente* and play cards, and the women—I tell you, amigo, my woman, Elena, she has friends that will . . ." He kissed his fingertips by way of showing their superior qualities. "They will see to your every need, and I mean your *every* need."

"We got to *get* to Arispe first," Cherokee Bill pointed out.

Joe tried to joke again. "There you go, Bill. Always thinking the worst."

"I'm being realistic," Bill said. The breed had

an enormous head and huge, square hands. He rarely smiled, and his dark eyes peered threateningly from under shaggy brows. "These horses ain't going to make Arispe. They ain't even going to make the border."

Gus was unworried. "Well, if you lunkheads had been using your eyes more and running your mouths less, you'd've noticed longhorn sign in the thickets hereabouts."

Virge looked puzzled. "You want us to ride cows to Mexico?"

"Where there's cattle, there must be a ranch," Gus explained patiently, "and where there's a ranch, there's . . . horses."

The bandits brightened. Not long after, a distant line of cottonwoods and willows gave evidence of a stream. Approaching the stream, the bandits topped a small rise. Below them, just upstream, was a ranch.

It was a small spread. There couldn't have been more than one or two hands, plus the owner. There was an adobe house, with a sod and brush roof and a rack of steer horns over the door. Behind the house was a lean-to, where the help slept; and beside the house was a ramada with saddles and other tack in its shade. There was a corral with about a dozen horses inside, and farther along two men were building a cattle pen from mesquite logs. The scene seemed quiet and peaceful in the afternoon heat.

Gus looked at his men and smiled. "Let's go down and say howdy do."

GUS AND HIS MEN RODE SLOWLY DOWN THE slope toward the ranch.

The horses in the corral began whinnying. The two men working on the cattle pen looked up. They stopped what they were doing and came forward, wiping their sweaty faces with bandannas. One stopped to drink water from a bucket.

In front of the ranch house the five bandits halted. Their horses stank of sweat. Two were red with blood. Joe Crist slumped in his saddle, holding his crudely bandaged shoulder. Around them the wind whispered through the cottonwood and willow leaves. The shallow stream murmured gently over its rocky bed. In the corral the ranch horses neighed and blew and pranced around.

The men from the corral came up. The first was young, with sandy hair and a boyishly enthusiastic smile. The one behind him looked even younger. "Morning, boys," said the first man.

Gus looked around, his dark eyes missing nothing. "Morning."

"Looks like you could use a little help," said the ranchman.

"Yeah," Gus replied. "We had us a run-in with Apaches about ten miles back."

The young ranchman didn't believe them, but he didn't want trouble. "We'll do anything we can. I'm Jim McNally. This is my hand, Bert Cooper."

The young cowboy, Bert, nodded nervously to the newcomers. With Paco he helped Joc from his horse, and they laid him in the shade of a willow tree.

The rest of the bandits dismounted. As they did so the ranch-house door opened, and a dark-haired woman appeared, wearing a blue gingham dress.

Proudly Jim McNally said, "This is my wife, Beth."

A light came into Gus's eyes. He doffed his hat, flashing the white smile that had charmed so many women before. "Afternoon, ma'am."

"Good afternoon," said Beth McNally with shy formality. She was slender and wiry, with rich, full lips. She could not have been out west long, because her creamy skin had not yet turned rough under the desert sun. Her hands were red from washing dishes, and she dried them on her apron.

Behind Gus, Virge Harper chuckled, "Howdy, miss." Paco Lopez removed his sombrero as a sign of respect, while Cherokee Bill just glowered.

Jim McNally said, "These men have had some trouble, Beth."

But Beth was already kneeling beside young Joe. "You've been shot," she said.

"Yes, ma'am," said Joe.

"Indians did it," Jim explained quickly, and as his wife's eyes met his own he flashed a warning look for her to go along with the story. Then, because he thought he should show more interest, he said to Gus, "Are the Indians still after you?"

Gus drank from the water bucket that hung from one of the adobe house's gallery awning supports. He shook his head as he passed the tin ladle to Virge. "They had enough of us."

While Beth cleaned Joe's wound and the rest of his men drank, Gus studied the small, tidy ranch. "Nice place," he said. "Been here long, Jim?"

"About a year, is all. We're still getting straightened out. We've been selling some of our beef to the army, the rest in San Miguel."

Gus nodded, eyes still moving. "Anybody else around?"

"N-no," Jim said, with a note of wariness in his voice.

Gus looked surprised. "No kids?"

Jim McNally fell for Gus's charm. "Naw." He

toed the dusty ground with his boot, and he cast a shy glance at his wife. "We been working on it, but no luck yet."

Gus took a turn around the ranch yard, as if he found all this very satisfactory.

Jim, who now believed these men would move on without trouble, said, "Where are you fellows headed, anyway?"

"Mexico," Gus replied.

"Lookin' to buy cattle?"

"Lookin' to get away from the law. We robbed us a bank."

Before Jim could react, Gus drew his pistol and shot him twice. The surprised young rancher cried out and crumpled to the ground.

Bert, the hand, turned and tried to run, but Virge and Cherokee Bill opened up on him, and he sprawled in the dust on his face.

McNally's wife, Beth, stood up from where she had been working on Joe. Her face was filled with shock; one hand went to her mouth involuntarily.

Gus turned toward her. He twirled his revolver and holstered it. Grinning, he advanced on her.

"No," she pleaded tearfully. "No."

She turned and raced for the house. Gus dashed after her, followed by Virge Harper.

Inside the door Beth snatched her husband's shotgun from the wall. With a smoothness she had not known she possessed, she thumbed back the hammers. She turned and raised the weapon, but before she could fire it, Gus snatched it from her hands. Beth uttered a little cry. Still grinning, Gus passed the shotgun back to Virge, who eased down the hammers.

Trembling, Beth retreated to the dark inside of the ranch house. Gus followed her.

Each of the bandits took a turn with her. Afterward, they stood in the doorway of the adobe house. Gus had borne the brunt of her resistance, and his face and neck were scratched and bleeding. The wounds seemed to excite him; a strange light still burned in his eyes. Next to him Virge giggled like a schoolboy hearing his first dirty joke. Paco brushed his sombrero, looking thoughtful. Cherokee Bill, who had gone last, buttoned his cheap wool trousers.

Gus turned back inside. Beth McNally lay on the floor, sobbing, with a thin blanket over her to cover her shame. Her face and one eye were bruised. Her lips were swollen. Her dark hair was pulled askew. The remains of the blue gingham dress were wadded nearby.

Gus grabbed her wrist and yanked her to her feet. She gave a little cry and tried to hide her nakedness with the blanket. "Get dressed," Gus told her. "You're coming with us."

"All right!" Virge chortled, slapping his thigh with glee.

Paco and Bill looked at each other. Bill said, "I don't like this, Gus. It's a mistake. She'll slow us down."

"That's all right," Gus said. He smiled lazily at

the brutalized woman. "I like it slow." Virge giggled some more, adding counterpoint to Beth's sobs.

Bill said, "We had our fun with her. Let's just kill her and be done with it."

Paco protested. "We have killed enough today, amigo. Why can't we just leave her here?"

"Because I said she's coming," Gus told them in a harsh voice. Then his anger subsided. "She's a fine woman, and I ain't had enough of her yet."

"Me neither," chorused Virge.

Gus moved back to Beth and slapped her bruised face. "I told you to get dressed. Now do it, and be quick about it."

Beth stumbled around, looking for fresh clothes. Satisfied, Gus led his men outside. Sweat ran into the cuts on his face and made them sting. He winced and dabbed his cheek. To his men he said, "Take the six best horses from the corral. Saddle five and put a pack on the other. Kill the rest."

"Kill them?" said Paco.

"That way nobody'll have fresh horses to chase us," Gus explained. "I don't like it, either, but that's the way it's got to be. Get some grain from the barn and put it on the packhorse. Whatever food and liquor you can find in the house, too—and their money, if they have any. We'll fill our water bags from the stream."

Virge didn't sound hopeful. "Bet they won't have much booze. They don't look like the type."

Gus shrugged. "You got enough money now, you can buy your own distillery when we get to Arispe."

Paco put on his sombrero. "Wait a minute," he said. "You said to saddle five horses. If the woman is coming, there will be six of us."

"No, there won't," Gus said.

He moved under the shade of the willow tree and looked down at Joe Crist. Joe stared back, and his voice was worried, afraid. "You're leaving me here, ain't you?"

Gus drew his pistol. "I wish we could, kid."

Paco cried, "Gus!"

"He can't keep up," Gus said, "and he knows who we are. The law's coming. If they get hold of him, he'll talk."

"No, Gus, I won't," Joe promised. "I swear, I won't."

"You think you won't now, but you will. They always do. I don't want my name on no posters in this territory. I got me enough trouble in Texas." He raised the pistol.

"Gus, no!" cried Joe.

Gus put the pistol barrel to Joe's forehead and pulled the trigger. The young man jerked and fell back.

"Life's a bitch," Gus remarked.

The bandits looked on. Paco was stunned. One of his legs was shaking. What had just happened was awful. Cherokee Bill was emotionless. He regarded Joe's death as a practical necessity. He didn't see why Gus had stuck with the kid this long. Virge was ambivalent. He had liked Joe, but this made one less way to split the bank loot.

"Don't stand there gaping," Gus told them. "Get the woman and let's get going."

"EASY ON THAT WATER," SAM WARNED.

Carolyn Manning lowered her canteen, surprised. "I thought you said there's a stream not far from here."

"In this country you never take anything for granted. That's how you stay alive. That stream might be dried up. It probably won't be, but it *might* be. Or we might get jumped and have to hole up. Treat water like you don't know where your next drink is coming from—'cause you probably don't."

Sam and Carolyn were following the trail left by the bandits and Sheriff Carpenter's posse. They kept as fast a pace as Sam thought possible without using up their horses. Sam had bought the best horses he could find in town. They didn't have speed, but they had bottom, the kind of animals that could grind out the miles.

Carolyn sat her mount easily. Her corduroy riding skirt had been slit up the middle, then sewn together to form legs and reinforced with buckskin to prevent chafing. "I was right," she announced, in the tone of a person who is used to being right, "Grissom and his gang *are* headed for Mexico, aren't they?"

"Far as I can tell they are," Sam grunted. "Nothing else in this direction, 'cept maybe the South Pole."

"Will we catch them?"

Sam thought about the forty-five hundred dollars that she had offered him for the gang's elimination, and there was a sinking feeling in his stomach. "I don't see how we can. Our only hope is that Grissom crosses the border before the posse catches him. The posse has to turn back at the border—I don't."

"You mean, *we* don't," she corrected.

Sam grit his teeth and went on. "Unfortunately for us, those bandits have at least two hurt horses. They'll be lucky to get to the border, much less beat Sheriff Carpenter across it."

"Can't we go around?" she said. "Cut them off somehow?"

Sam shook his head. "They're headed for Dead Horse Pass. I know this country. There's no shortcuts to the pass. So, unless something unexpected happens, this is likely to be a wild-goose chase for us."

"Grissom and his men could get caught by the posse and shoot their way out," Carolyn suggested hopefully.

"There is that possibility," Sam admitted. Then he said, "You really want to get them yourself, don't you?"

"I told you that before."

"And after you get your revenge, what then?"

"Who knows?" she said, as if that were the farthest thing from her mind.

"It's not good to live for revenge, Miss Manning. It eats you up inside. It'll change you, and not for the better. Sometimes it's best just to forget and get on with your life."

"I can't forget, Mr. Slater. I can't, and I won't."

Sam shook his head. "You're one hardheaded woman. You got any idea what you could be getting yourself into, if we do catch Grissom and his gang?"

"Oh, please—don't start this again."

"I'm starting again 'cause it's true. People are liable to get hurt, hurt bad. This is work for a professional, and it's best done by a professional—alone."

"Then maybe you'd better start thinking of me as a professional."

"I give up trying to talk sense to you. I'll say one thing in your favor—you're keeping up better than I expected."

"There was never any doubt about that," she said.

The sun was well into the west when Sam and Carolyn reached the stream. They topped the ridge and saw the ranch below them. Even at this distance they could make out a half-dozen dead horses in the corral and two more in front of the adobe ranch house. They could make out newly dug graves behind the house as well. The stench of death wafted up to them—a smell that was all too familiar to Sam.

They exchanged glances, and Sam drew his saddle gun. "Stay here," he told Carolyn.

"I most certainly will not," she said.

"Have it your way, then," he said, and they started down the slope.

Flies buzzed in huge clouds around the dead horses as Sam and Carolyn rode up. Black, congealed blood stained the sand beneath the horses' heads. Sam and Carolyn breathed through their mouths to lessen the effects of the smell.

Sam dismounted warily, holding the saddle gun. The ranch-house door was ajar. Sam poked it open the rest of the way with his rifle barrel and stepped in. The house was wrecked; it had been rifled for anything of value. Sam looked in the lean-to out back. Two people had lived in the house, he determined, with a hand in the lean-to.

He came back to where Carolyn waited with the horses. "Grissom's been here, all right. Looks like they killed most of the people here and took fresh horses. Then they killed the rest of the horses so the posse wouldn't be able to use them. Carpenter and his men must have stayed long enough to bury the victims."

He waited for a reaction from Carolyn. "I'd have expected you to be more squeamish about this."

"You forget, I've seen men killed before. It tends to harden one. I do feel sorry for them, of course. I feel sorry for these poor animals as well."

"Killing the horses was a smart move on Grissom's part. This changes everything. Makes it a lot less likely Carpenter and his men can catch the gang before they cross the border."

Carolyn brightened. "Then we'll—we'll get a chance at them after all?"

"Maybe."

Still keeping a wary eye, Sam examined the shallow graves. Each was surmounted with a rough wooden cross. They bore inscriptions carved with a knife: "Jim McNally," "Bert Cooper," and "Unknown."

"McNally, Cooper—either of them part of Grissom's gang?" Sam asked Carolyn.

She shook her head. "Not that I'm aware."

Sam nodded. "One of the gang was wounded. He must have died, one way or the other, and be buried in this third grave." He mounted his horse. "You fill the water bags and canteens, I'm going for a scout."

He returned a bit later, dismounting and taking a drink from his canteen. "I been reading sign. What I've seen confirmed what I thought when I looked in the house. There was a woman living here, and Grissom and his men have taken her with them."

"A hostage?" Carolyn speculated.

"Something like that. The rancher's wife, I reckon."

"The dirty . . ." Carolyn said. Then she added, "I feel sorry for any woman unfortunate enough to be a prisoner of Gus Grissom."

Sam didn't say anything. Before, he hadn't thought there was much chance of catching Grissom. Now it was a distinct possibility. If Grissom was holding a female hostage, it was only going to make things that much more difficult. What was Sam going to do with Carolyn Manning when the lead started to fly? He tapped his saddle thoughtfully.

After they had watered and rested the horses, they pushed on, to use what remained of the light. They made camp that evening in a secluded, brush-filled draw. Sam watered the horses from the oiled canvas bags. He staked them out to graze, then hobbled them for the night well down the draw. He gathered dried brush for a fire.

"Aren't you going to hunt game?" Carolyn said. "I'm certain there's an abundance of rabbits here, if nothing else."

"Can't risk gunshots," Sam told her. "We don't know who's around."

"You mean Apaches? But they're not supposed to be—"

"Like I said, out here you don't take chances. That's how you stay alive."

Sam dug a hole, put the brush in, and started a small fire, screened by the rocks so that its smoke couldn't be seen more than a few feet away. To Carolyn the fire appeared too small for cooking, but Sam boiled a pot of coffee, then fried some jerky and bread, heated canned beans, and opened some canned fruit.

"Coffee?" he said, holding out the pot.

She let him fill her cup. "Thank you."

"You look more like a tea drinker to me," Sam said.

"I was, once, but I've learned to appreciate coffee since I came west. There really hasn't been much choice."

Sam opened a packet of *peloncillo,* Mexican brown sugar, and they each put some in their coffee. The drinks were hot, sweet, and refreshing. Carolyn sat cross-legged on the ground. Sam leaned against his saddle while he ate. Above them the setting sun streaked the desert sky purple and gold.

Hunger got the best of Carolyn's manners, and she gobbled down everything on her plate. "That was good," she said, as though she found it hard to believe that Sam could prepare anything edible.

She set down her plate and relaxed, sipping a second cup of coffee. "In San Miguel they say you're part Apache, Mr. Slater."

"Blood brother," Sam corrected.

"How thrilling. What is that like?"

Sam shrugged. "I'm an adopted member of the tribe. No need to make more of it than there is."

"But it's so . . . so exotic. I read in *Harper's* about Mr. Jefford and Cochise, how they mingled their blood in that barbaric Indian ritual."

Sam laughed without humor. "Apaches think that white men are the barbarians."

Carolyn couldn't believe that. "Really?"

"Really."

"You almost sound as though you agree with them."

"I do."

Darkness had fallen. Somewhere a coyote began to howl, and was answered by another. Coyote the Trickster, the Apaches called him. You couldn't get away from those damn animals. They were everywhere. If men ever got to the moon, Sam expected they'd find that coyotes had gotten there first.

"Who adopted you?" Carolyn said, interrupting his thoughts.

"Chiricahua," Sam told her. "Bedonkhe band."

"No, I mean what Indian? Was he a chief, like Cochise?"

"Yes. I can't say his name, though."

"Why not?"

"Apache custom. You're not allowed to speak the name of a dead man."

"But you're not a real Apache. Surely it makes no difference to you."

"A part of me's Apache." He tapped his chest. "A part in here. And that part would never do anything against the laws of the tribe. My Apache father kept me from being killed. When they caught me, I was fifteen, an age where they might have put me to death, especially since I was big for my age. But my father talked them out of it. He saw something in me that he liked, and he persuaded them to adopt me into the tribe. In a lot of ways he meant more to me than my real father. I certainly knew him better."

"Why? What happened to your real father?"

"He was killed in a Sioux raid, in Montana, along with the rest of my family. It happened when I was just a toddler. I was brought up by . . . by an uncle."

"You're a long way from Montana," Carolyn said.

"Yeah."

He didn't tell her that he was wanted for murder in Montana—for the murder of the same uncle who had raised him. He remembered his uncle's uncontrolled drinking, and how he'd tried to rape his own daughter, Lucinda. Sam had come to Lucinda's defense. In the knife fight that had followed, Sam had gotten the scar that he would carry to the grave, and his uncle had gotten—the grave.

"Tell me," Carolyn went on, "whatever possesses a man to become a bounty hunter?"

"You ask a lot of questions, lady."

"I'm curious," she said.

Sam stared into his coffee. "I guess some

people just aren't cut out for anything else."

He tossed the dregs of the coffee onto the ground and stood. "We better turn in. Long day tomorrow."

Carolyn rose. She took an unused stick of firewood, tested its point, then drew a line with it down the middle of their tiny camp.

"What is *that*?" asked Sam.

With the stick Carolyn pointed to each side of the line in turn. "This is my side of the camp. That is your side. Kindly remain on your side for the duration of the night."

Sam stared.

Carolyn went on. "I don't want you to think that being alone together like this gives you a license to approach me physically."

"Lady, I'd rather tangle with a wildcat," Sam said. He picked up his rifle. "I'll stand first guard."

"Guard?"

"That's right. Out here you've got to keep a lookout, if you—"

"If you want to stay alive. Yes, yes, I know."

Carolyn was more tired than she had realized. She wrapped herself in her blankets and lay down near the tiny fire, resting her head on her saddle.

Sam looked down at her and grinned. "Comfy?"

"Mm," she mumbled. Her eyes were closed; she was already half-asleep.

"I'll wake you when it's your turn for guard."

"Mm."

Carolyn slept well and deeply. When at last

she opened her eyes, the birds were singing and the sun was coming up.

Carolyn sat up and looked around. Sam was nowhere in sight. His saddle and the rest of his gear were gone.

She threw off her blanket and stood. She looked down the draw. Sam's horse and the packhorse were missing as well. Sam had left her and gone after Gus Grissom on his own.

"Damn."

Carolyn fumed, fists on her hips, thin lips compressed. She stamped the ground in anger and frustration. She looked around for a suitable target, then kicked her Spanish-style hat across the camp. After that she kicked her saddle.

"Damn!" She said it again.

Gradually she calmed down. Sam had left her horse and plenty of supplies, more than enough for her to get back to San Miguel. She had a quick breakfast, then she saddled the horse and started off—after Sam.

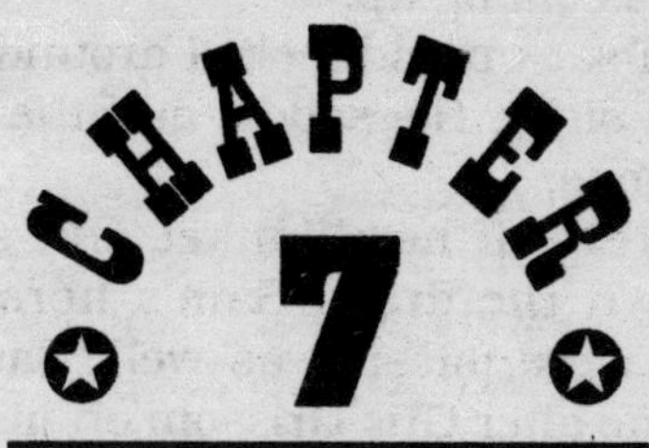

DEAD HORSE PASS HAD GOTTEN ITS NAME from the animal that the first white man to venture there had found. It was a narrow, twisted opening in a range of cactus-covered hills that rose abruptly from the desert basin. Not far from the pass's entrance, a gully ran nearly parallel to the hills. The gully was filled with the same brush and cactus that covered the basin, and it was invisible to a man on horseback until he was within twenty yards of it.

Over the gully's rim peered an Apache Indian. There were two vermilion stripes across the Apache's cheeks. He had removed his shirt and tucked his long breechclout into his waistband in preparation for battle, as was customary among his people.

The Apache was lithe and unusually tall, so of course the Mexicans had called him Chiquito, or "Little One," though his real name was Nabi-jin-taha, meaning "He is Given Tests." In the gully with Chiquito were a dozen warriors, similarly painted and dressed. Their horses were hidden just inside the entrance to the pass. The Apaches were waiting to ambush a party of white men. They had crossed the white men's tracks yesterday. They had found their discarded tobacco sticks. They had seen their campfire while they had circled around and then had ridden all night to get to this place that Chiquito had selected for fighting.

Chiquito was the last living member of his family. His father had been murdered by treacherous Mexicans at what was supposed to have been a friendship feast. His brother had been killed by the *norteamericanos* in battle. His son had died from white man's disease, and his wife had been carried off by Mexicans to be a slave, or worse.

Once Chiquito's people had lived in the White Mountains, but they had been driven from there by white men seeking *oro-hay*, the yellow metal. The white men wanted Chiquito's people to live on what they called a "reservation"—a hot, airless desert where nothing grew and there was no game to hunt. The whites had sworn to provide them with food, but the provisions always arrived late, there was never as much as promised, and the quality was bad. On the reservation his people's health had deteriorated —that was where his son had died—and their spirit had withered, like the crops they had been encouraged to plant. Chiquito had decided that if he must die, it would be as a free man and warrior, not as a slave and prisoner. He had left the reservation and had been on the run ever since. Most of his original followers were gone, killed in battle or wounded and captured, but he had acquired new followers from other bands, men who had heard of him and who shared his desire to be free.

Chiquito's companions were spread along the gully, motionless under the blazing sun. They could lie that way for hours, no matter what the discomfort to themselves, stalking their prey, like the Tigers of the Desert that the Mexicans called them.

Suddenly Chiquito saw something in the distance, and his dark eyes gleamed. It was a column of dust, made by men on horseback, coming toward him. Slowly, so as not to disturb so much as a leaf, he eased his rifle—the barrel of which had been blackened to avoid reflecting sunlight—into firing position. He whispered down the gully. "Fill your hearts with courage, my friends. The enemy is coming."

Sheriff George Carpenter and the posse from San Miguel came on quickly, pushing their horses. Carpenter was motivated by deep rage. He had known Jim McNally and Bert Cooper—hell, they all had. There had been no need for the bandits to kill them. The posse members had all known Beth McNally, too, and they were consumed by fear about what had happened to her.

Before them rose a range of steep hills. Carpenter saw a break in them. Barnes, the leathery-faced cattleman, eased his horse alongside, pointing. "That's Dead Horse Pass."

Carpenter nodded.

"No sign of them bandits."

Carpenter nodded again. "I know. I'd hoped to catch them by now."

Just behind them the gambler Paget said, "We lost that chance when they stole Jim McNally's horses."

"Well, we're going to catch them," Carpenter promised. "We'll catch them if we have to kill our horses doing it."

"It looks like that just might happen, too," Barnes said. The rancher was worried about his mount's condition. The horse was a favorite of his.

Carpenter went on. "You read sign, Barnes. How far behind them are we?"

"An hour, hour and a half."

"And the border?"

"Ten miles, after the pass."

Paget, who had fought Mosby's guerrillas during the war, said, "They must have seen our dust by now. They must know we're coming."

"You thinking what I'm thinking?" asked

Vickery, the heavyset miner, who was riding beside Paget.

"Yeah," said Paget. "If they're going to turn and ambush us, it'll be in that pass."

Carpenter agreed. Raising his voice above the noise of the horses, he called down the column. "Keep your eyes peeled for trouble, boys."

He needn't have said it. Every man's eye was on the approaching pass. There was something ominous about it, forbidding. They searched the pass's steep sides, looking for movement, looking for the reflection of sunlight off gun metal.

Carpenter had been thinking about something for a while. Now he voiced his idea to the rest of the posse. "You know, if we don't catch these bastards at the border, I'll be tempted to put away my badge and cross into Mexico after them."

"If you do, I'll go with you," said Barnes.

"Me too," added Carpenter's young deputy, Ed Burke.

"Anybody else?" asked Carpenter.

"Me," said Paget.

"And me," said Vickery. The other members of the posse volunteered as well.

Barnes said, "We're agreed, then. What worries me is what will happen to Beth when the fighting starts."

Grimly Sheriff Carpenter said, "What worries me is what will happen to her if—"

His words were drowned out by a burst of gunfire from right in front of them. The firing seemed to come out of the very earth. Animals reared, men toppled from their horses. Other men struggled to control their mounts while they drew rifles and pistols and fired at the unseen enemy.

Carpenter's first thought was that it must be the bandits, but the cattleman Barnes remembered the gully, and he yelled, "Apaches! Right in front—" Then he went down, falling off his horse with the lower part of his jaw shot away.

The firing continued. The Apaches could not be seen in the dust and powder smoke. Vickery, the Regular Army veteran, had been ambushed by Indians before. "Charge them!" he yelled. "Right into them, it's the only way!" He spurred his reluctant horse toward the unseen foe, firing his rifle at the muzzle flashes in the brush. Then his horse was shot and fell. Vickery rolled out from under the falling beast. Smoke and dust obscured his vision. He picked up his rifle and fired it at the brush-filled gully, then a bullet caught him in the chest and he fell, near his still-thrashing horse.

Tony Forrest, the young hardware merchant, lost control of his horse. As it ran away he threw himself off of it. He landed hard, breaking his leg. Crying with pain, he tried to crawl away, but a bullet hit him in the back, breaking his spine. He lay with his face in the dirt, helpless, wishing he had never come here, hoping that he died before the Apaches got to him.

Sheriff Carpenter's men were going down all around him. His only desire was to get at least some of them to safety. He looked around and saw a small hillock off to his right.

"Get to that hill," he cried, pointing. "Come on, boys."

What was left of the posse rode off. Carpenter's horse was shot, stumbled, and went down. Carpenter hit the ground and came up spitting dirt. Ed Burke rode up beside him, shifting in the saddle and offering a hand. "Come on!"

Carpenter swung up behind the deputy, and they started for the hill. Those two and Paget were the only ones left. Carpenter hoped to reach the hill and take cover in the rocks there. Their tired horses could never outrace the Apaches across the desert, especially with him riding double; but if they could make a stand in the rocks, the Indians might get discouraged and leave them alone.

The gambler Paget was hit just below the shoulder blade; he reeled in the saddle. His horse misstepped on a patch of uneven ground, and he fell off. He rose unsteadily. Ed Burke wheeled his own horse to try to help, but Paget waved him off. "Go on. I'll catch up."

Burke and Carpenter made for the hill. Paget followed, gritting his teeth, trying to ignore his wound. The Apaches were out of the gully now, howling in triumph, finishing off the wounded. Paget turned and fired his pistol at them, hoping to slow them up. He thought he hit one. Then he was shot again, in the hip. He staggered and sat heavily in the dirt, swearing. The Apaches were still coming on. He fired, but his pistol was empty. He reloaded, trying to ignore the Apaches racing toward him. The screaming Apaches were almost on him. He didn't have time to put six bullets into the pistol. He shut the loading gate and raised the weapon to fire. He squeezed off a wild round, and then the Indians were on him with clubs and knives. . . .

Ed Burke and Sheriff Carpenter reached the hillock. They half fell, half slid off the horse and took cover in the jumbled rocks. The horse ran away, but they paid it no notice as bullets screamed off the rocks around them. Feverishly they reloaded their pistols. Carpenter's rifle had been lost with the horses. In his excitement Ed had forgotten to take it from his saddle when he dismounted.

Suddenly the firing stopped. There was silence. The dust cleared, the haze of powder smoke blew away. The Apaches were nowhere to be seen. There were just the bodies of the other posse members, pale in the sun where they had been stripped. It was quiet. There was no singing of birds, no rustle of small animals in the undergrowth. In all that expanse of desert, the only movement came from the wounded horses. The good horses had been spirited away, seemingly into thin air.

Ed Burke was hatless. His fair hair hung in a mop over his forehead as he licked his lips. "I'm scared, Sheriff."

"Moi aussi, mon fils. Moi aussi."

"What?"

"Nothing. I'm scared, too, son. And call me George."

The young deputy brightened. "All right . . . George. What's going to happen now?"

"I don't know, son. I don't know." Carpenter rubbed the back of the boy's head as a form of reassurance.

"I don't want them to take me alive."

"Neither do I."

There was a noise in the underbrush before them.

"What was that, George?" said Ed.

Before Carpenter could answer, there was a shot, and a bullet zipped between them.

Carpenter cocked his pistol. "Here they come."

"AGAIN?" SAID GUS GRISSOM IN DISBELIEF.

Virge Harper chuckled and scratched his unshaven cheek. "Ain't had me a woman in a while. I reckon I got the itch."

"I don't know what 'Virge' stands for, but it sure ain't for 'virgin,'" cracked the giant breed, Cherokee Bill.

Virge busted up laughing at that. The four bandits and their prisoner, Beth McNally, were halted at the far end of Dead Horse Pass. Paco, the Mexican, complained. "How many times you going to let him have her, Gus? He is holding us up."

"It's all right," said Virge. "We got us a big lead on that posse, if there is a posse."

"There's a posse," Gus assured him.

Virge was insistent. "You said she belonged to all of us. You said we could have her whenever we wanted."

"I didn't think you'd want her this much. You're worse than a damn dog, Virge."

Virge's insistence turned to anger. "Goddammit, Gus. I got the right."

At last Gus said, "All right, take her up in them rocks. You probably won't be more than two or three minutes, anyway." Paco laughed at that, and Gus went on. "The rest of us will grab a break."

Virge chuckled again. He slid from his horse, then pulled Beth McNally from hers. Beneath her bruises and cuts Beth's once creamy face was sunburned and peeling. No one had thought to bring her a hat. Her swollen lips were cracked and black with dried blood. She was unused to riding, and her saddle and the inside of her thighs were splotched with blood from her blistered skin. Her dark hair was tangled and matted with dirt.

She didn't resist as Virge dragged her into the rocks. She had learned to submit quietly. At first she had cried all the time, but now she had stopped. It had all become a blur to her. It was like she wasn't there anymore. Only her body was present. Her soul and spirit were gone.

The other three bandits loosened their saddle girths and waited in the scant shade of the rocks. It was quiet save for Virge's scrapings and moanings of pleasure behind them.

Gus wasn't happy with the way Virge was trying to take over the McNally woman. He didn't mind sharing her, but this was ridiculous. Nearby, Paco twirled his long pigtail around one finger. Paco was very vain about his hair. He untied it, brushed and oiled it every night. Cherokee Bill stared into space, his huge hands clasped together. After that first time neither Paco nor Bill had taken the girl again, which was just as well with Gus.

Gus's prediction had been accurate—Virge did not take long. When he was done, he dragged the McNally woman back. The woman slumped to the ground, where Gus gave her a canteen of water and a tortilla. He didn't want her to die.

Virge was full of himself. The brushy little blond beard under his lip seemed to puff out with pride, like a cockscomb. To Gus he said, "Was it like this when you rode with Quantrill?"

Gus snorted. "Are you kidding? Quantrill treated women like they was goddesses. He didn't care what you did to the men, but he'd shoot you if you so much as looked sideways at a woman."

"Well, he'd've had his hands full with this outfit, that's for sure," Virge crowed.

Gus looked sour. "You wouldn't have lasted five minutes with Quantrill."

Virge let the insult pass. He stretched his skinny frame luxuriously, like a cat in the sun. This was the kind of life he'd envisioned when he'd thrown in with Grissom, back in Fort

Griffin. The money was good and the work was sure easier than getting your ribs stove in by some crazed steer or half-broke saddle bronc.

"Quantrill, I guess he taught you everything, huh?" Virge asked Gus.

"Him and some others," Gus replied. Truth was, Gus had learned his current trade from a pair of Quantrill's boys, the James brothers. They'd showed him the profitability of robbing banks, but they'd made Kansas and Missouri too hot for that kind of activity, so Gus had drifted south, to Texas, where pickings were easier. There hadn't been much else for him to do after the war. His parents' farm had been burned out by Redlegs, and the land confiscated and given to a Unionist. The Yankees had killed his brother, a grudge that Gus would never forgive. His parents and sister had tried to rebuild elsewhere, but Gus wasn't much on rebuilding. It was too much like work. Gus had grown footloose during the war, and that was a hard habit to break. Right now he was tired, though, and looking forward to a stay in Mexico. With his share of the bank loot and some money he'd stolen off a whore in Fort Griffin he should be set up right well.

Virge eyed Beth McNally again. "What are we going to do with her when we get to Tamaleville, or whatever you call this place we're headed?"

"It is called Arispe," said Paco, stiffening with pride.

"I figured we'd sell her to the Mexes," Gus

told Virge. "Woman like her'd fetch a pretty price for their whorehouses."

Gus's words seemed to have no impact on Beth, but Virge looked disappointed, and Gus said, "Why? Don't tell me you want to keep her?"

"Maybe," said Virge.

"And do what? Settle down and marry her?"

Paco and Cherokee Bill hooted at the thought. Virge looked defensive, and Gus said, "You'll be able to buy all the women you want in Arispe."

"I want her," Virge said. "Besides, I ain't got to pay for her. I never had me a woman I ain't had to pay for."

"Well, don't get used to it, 'cause you ain't keepin' this one."

"You're giving a lot of orders," Virge said defiantly.

Gus stood. "I think you've forgot who's boss here."

"I ain't scared of you," Virge said, and his hand dropped to his pistol.

Gus's voice grew deadly quiet. "Maybe you better get scared."

Before Virge could reply, there was the not-too-distant sound of gunshots. All heads turned, even Beth's.

Paco and Cherokee Bill stood, along with Gus and Virge. The gunfire came from just beyond the unseen head of the pass, about a mile distant. It reached a crescendo, its reports filtering back through the narrow walls of the pass.

"What is it?" said Virge.

"The posse," Gus whispered. "It's got to be."

For a moment there was life in Beth's blue eyes, then it faded as Paco said, "The Apaches have caught them." He crossed himself. "The poor men."

"How'd they get so close to us?" Virge wondered in surprise. "They must've burned up their horses."

"They won't be burning nothing, after this," Gus said. He looked at Beth, who slumped once more, refusing to meet his eyes. Already the gunfire had begun to fade. Now it was just scattered shots.

Paco was scared. "That could have been us."

"Yeah, but it ain't," Gus said. He started for the horses. "Come on, let's put some miles between us and them Injuns."

Sam saw the vultures from a long way off. There were a lot of them, circling, swooping low.

Sam's throat went dry. He drew his saddle gun, shifting uneasily. He'd crossed Indian sign early this morning and had been worried about it ever since. He was more than ever glad that he'd gotten rid of Carolyn Manning. He hoped she'd had sense enough to go back to San Miguel. Sam intended to deal with the Grissom gang by himself and bring back their bodies. Carolyn would raise a stink and run off at the mouth about it, but in the end she'd pay the promised rewards.

As Sam drew closer to whatever it was the vultures were feasting on, he dismounted and ground-hitched his horse and packhorse in a fold of earth. Carrying the rifle, he eased his way up the rise for a look-see.

Scattered through the brush and cactus he made out the bodies of men and horses, with the vultures picking at them. He smelled flesh bloating in the sun.

He hung his head. There were too many bodies for it to be the Grissom gang. It could only be the posse. They must have been jumped by Apaches, probably the bunch led by that war chief called Chiquito. Sam watched for a while, motionless. When he had satisfied himself that there was no one around, he remounted and rode closer.

It was the posse, all right. They had been stripped and robbed of their possessions. Sam recognized some of their faces despite the clouds of flies and the mutilations of the Apaches. The horses snorted and tried to shy away, but Sam curbed them. The vultures flapped their wings lazily, little disturbed by Sam's presence. A few flew away, but most continued gorging themselves or simply hopped to the next body.

Sam saw Tony Forrest, the prosperous-looking young man who had wanted him to come with the posse. If Sam had gone, maybe these men wouldn't be dead now. On the other hand, maybe Sam would be lying there with them, sliced to pieces. Either way there was nothing he could do about it.

A quick glance around told what had happened. The Indians had hidden in the gully and sprung their ambush when the posse was just yards away. Sam saw where some of the men had retreated toward a nearby hillock. He found one man, the handsome fellow who looked like a gunman, halfway to the hill with his head smashed open. Tracks of a horse ridden double kept going in that direction. Sam followed them until he came upon two more bodies in the rocks.

The bodies belonged to Sheriff Carpenter and that young deputy of his, Ed. Their weapons were gone, but from the position of the bodies and the wounds, it looked like they had simultaneously shot one another in the mouth to avoid being taken alive. That was why they hadn't been stripped or carved up. Apaches believed it was bad medicine to take one's own life, and they wouldn't touch someone who had done it.

Sam wiped a hand across his scarred face. He had left a dead man in Carpenter's chair. It didn't seem like much of a joke now.

Sam squatted by the bodies, rifle cradled in his arms. He looked back the way he had come. Carolyn Manning had probably gone back to town. But what if she hadn't? What if she was out there, alone, with Chiquito and his warriors on the loose?

It was a chance Sam couldn't take.

He sipped a little water from his canteen, trying to wash the taste of death from his mouth. Then he remounted his horse and started back the way he had come. His eyes never stopped moving. There was a hollow feeling in the pit of his stomach.

He had not gone more than three miles when he spotted a distant plume of dust—a single rider, coming toward him out of the shimmering heat haze. Gradually a figure appeared in the dust, and he recognized the flat, Spanish-style hat and expensive riding outfit of Carolyn Manning.

Sam dismounted, to rest his horse and wait. Carolyn drew up to him. Heat and dirt had wilted her clothes, but she was as overbearing as ever. In her broad accent she said, "You seem to have forgotten something when you broke camp this morning, Mr. Slater."

"What's that?"

"Me."

"I didn't forget you," Sam said.

"You were hoping you had gotten rid of me."

"I was hoping that for once you'd do the intelligent thing and go back to San Miguel, but knowing you, I should have expected different. Well, this is your lucky day, Miss Manning."

"Why?"

"Because I came back for you."

"I presume you had a guilty conscience?"

"No, I thought I'd try and keep you alive."

Sam remounted and took up the packhorse's lead line. Looking smug, Carolyn said, "What changed your mind?"

"You'll see."

They rode on in silence, until they came to the massacre site.

Carolyn turned sickly pale. "What—what is it?"

"The posse from San Miguel," Sam told her. "They found those Apaches that ain't supposed to be around here."

The smell had grown so bad that Sam pulled up his bandanna and Carolyn held a handkerchief to her nose. "Now you see why I came back for you," Sam said.

They skirted around the bodies, barely disturbing the vultures. Carolyn pulled up her horse. "Wait. Those men—aren't you going to stop and bury them?"

"Nope."

"Why?"

"No time."

"You're certainly not much of a Christian, Mr. Slater."

"I never professed to be one, Miss Manning. You bury them if you want, I'm going on."

He rode ahead. Carolyn hesitated, then followed him.

AS SAM AND CAROLYN APPROACHED DEAD Horse Pass, Sam read the sign. The Apaches who had ambushed the posse had gone into the pass afterward. They'd probably hidden their horses there. The tracks of Grissom's gang were visible as well. Had the Apaches gone after the bandits next? It was likely, Sam thought. Or could it be that they were laying an ambush for someone else . . . ?

"Come on," he told Carolyn, turning away from the pass.

"What are you doing?" she said.

"I don't like this. We're going through the hills instead."

"We'll lose time."

"We'll still have time enough to catch Grissom and his gang before they reach Arispe. That's all we need."

Carolyn was doubtful as she looked at the rocky, cactus-covered hills looming above them. "Won't it be hard?"

"Probably," Sam told her.

They started into the hills. There was no trail, and the footing was uneven. Sam let his horse pick the way, only guiding the animal in the general direction he wanted.

"Ow!" said Carolyn, her cry breaking the stillness.

Sam looked back. Carolyn was near a clump of cholla cactus, holding her lower right leg.

"These needles, they—they jumped right out at me," she complained, sounding amazed.

"Cholla will do that," Sam observed.

"What do you suggest I do?"

"Don't get so close next time."

Carolyn plucked the needles from her leg. "Tell me, Mr. Slater, was this detour really necessary?"

Sam jerked a thumb toward the plain. "Ask those fellas back there," he said. Then he added, "It's not too much for you, is it?"

"I can go anywhere you can," Carolyn retorted.

"I hope so, Miss Manning. I hope so."

"You don't like me very much, do you?"

"I don't feel much about you one way or the other. I just aim to collect that reward you're offering."

They struggled on through the hills. There was no water, not at this time of year. They watered their horses from the oiled canvas bags on the packhorse's back. They spent much of their time leading the animals up steep slopes and down the far sides. Carolyn's clothes were shredded by cactus. She twisted her ankles on the rough ground.

"The horses seem to be a liability in these hills," she breathed at one point.

"That's what puts the cavalry at a disadvantage when they chase the Indians up here."

"What do the Apaches do with their horses here?"

Sam shrugged. "They eat them."

They were walking up a particularly steep grade. Carolyn fell further and further behind Sam. She strained to keep going. Sweat streamed off her forehead and matted her short red hair. Her thighs and calves burned with the pain of the climb, and that pain was reflected in her face. She was not used to so much walking, and she winced with each step of her blistered feet.

Near the top the going was almost vertical. Sam finished the climb first. He stopped and drank from his canteen, watching, seemingly unconcerned, as Carolyn struggled up the last incline. She held her horse's reins with one hand and grabbed on to rocks for support with the other, grunting with the effort.

At last she reached the top, with her horse

scrambling up behind her. She stood beside Sam, her chest heaving. "You might have given me a hand," she gasped.

"You looked like you were doing all right," Sam told her.

Rested, Sam looped the canteen over his saddle horn and started down the hill's far side. Carolyn gave a little cry of pain and followed after.

Late in the afternoon, after what seemed like forever to Carolyn, they left the hills. While Carolyn waited beneath the scant shade of a paloverde tree, Sam scouted ahead. Soon he returned.

"I picked up Grissom's trail," he told her.

"Any sign of the Apaches?"

"No."

"That's good," Carolyn said. Then she saw the look on his face, and she added, "Isn't it?"

Sam's eyes searched the horizon. "Maybe. Maybe not."

They rested and fed their horses, then pushed on. The land on this side of the pass was rolling and hilly, carpeted with cactus and brush. A man could see for twenty miles, but two hundred other men could hide within twenty feet of him. The rabbitbrush was just coming into flower, and in places it covered the plain with a yellow haze.

"I never imagined that a desert could look so colorful," Carolyn marveled.

"You should see it in the spring," Sam told her, "when the owl clover blooms in fields of pink, and the cactus are topped with red and yellow blossoms. It can be a pretty place."

"It's nothing like New Hampshire, that's for certain. Texas either."

"I don't know much about New Hampshire, but Texas is—" Sam stopped, reining in his horse, all his senses alert.

"What is it?" Carolyn said.

Sam didn't answer. He felt tingly all over. The hair on his arms and the back of his neck was standing straight up. He quartered the ground, but saw nothing. There was a low ridge off to their right, with another, higher ridge behind it. To the left the country was much the same. On the right-hand ridge, there was a high, rocky point, almost like a small tower. It would be the perfect spot for an Apache marksman to hide and . . .

Bang!

The bullet whizzed by Sam's face, galvanizing him to action. As the mounted warriors boiled over the crest of the ridge, he wheeled his horse and yelled to Carolyn, "Ride for it!"

The two of them galloped off, with the Apaches in pursuit. Sam had just enough time to glimpse the bare chests, the painted faces, and streaming dark hair. Sam and Carolyn galloped toward the next ridge line. Maybe they could find cover and make a stand. They leaned over their horses' necks; Sam hung on to the packhorse's lead. None of the animals was in good shape after the trek through the hills. Sam looked over his shoulder. The Indians were gaining.

Sam reined in his horse. Carolyn stopped as well, but Sam waved her on, "Keep going!"

Still holding the packhorse's lead, Sam drew his pistol. He aimed at the onrushing Indians and fired. He didn't hit anything, but the Apaches pulled up, wary of the white man's gun. Indians didn't take casualties if they could avoid it. They weren't like white men.

Carolyn was still riding hard, dust pluming behind her. While the Indians regrouped Sam started after her. Yelling from behind him told him that the Apaches were coming on again.

Carolyn reached the ridge. She lathered her horse up it and crested the top . . . to find another group of Apaches waiting for her.

Carolyn screamed as she rode into the Indians' midst. The Apaches reached out, grabbing for her bridle and reins. She quirted wildly to the right and left, momentarily driving them off, trying to wheel her horse to ride back down the hill.

"Ride through them!" Sam yelled, coming up behind her. He lashed out at one of the Apaches with his pistol barrel, catching the Indian on the side of the head. The Indian reeled and slumped in his wicker saddle. Sam let go the packhorse's lead. He grabbed Carolyn's bridle and led her down the hill with the Apaches right behind.

The big, grain-fed horses gave Sam and Carolyn an initial advantage in speed, but in the end the wiry Indian ponies, with their superior endurance, would run them down. They reached a flat stretch, spurring their mounts for all they were worth. Behind them some of the Apaches began shooting. Sam rode alongside Carolyn, beating her horse's rear with his hat, urging it to go faster. "Yah!" he cried. "Yah!"

They galloped flat out. Sam prayed that one of the horses didn't misstep or fall in a hole. The cactus tore Sam and Carolyn's legs and the legs of their horses, but they paid no attention.

They slid down the sides of a dry wash at a speed that should have killed them both. They turned up the wash, but were cut off by a group of Apaches who had circled around them. With difficulty they turned their mounts and urged them out of the wash.

Across the open ground they raced once more, with the Apaches ever closer. Their horses were flagging; they wouldn't go much farther. The Indian yells were loud in their ears. There was a humpbacked mountain to their front. Sam saw a cave near its base. He pointed out the cave to Carolyn, who understood. They spurred their faltering animals forward. A bullet creased Carolyn's shoulder and she cried out.

They reached the mountain. They raced their horses up the shale slope to the cave. They fell off the weary animals, beating them into the cave at the same time as Sam drew his rifle from its scabbard and Carolyn took her .45 carbine.

The Apaches were right behind them. There was no time to aim; they just pointed their weapons and fired. Sam downed the leading Apache, who bounced on the ground and lay still. Carolyn hit the second Indian's horse. The animal faltered, then fell, with its rider rolling free. As Sam and Carolyn fired at the man another Apache raced forward, took the downed warrior onto his horse's back and raced away, disappearing into the dry wash with the rest of the war party. Suddenly the Apaches were gone, almost as if they had never been there.

Sam looked at Carolyn, impressed. "You can shoot."

"Of course," she said, reloading the carbine. "Will they attack again?"

"I don't know." Sam looked at the fading sun. "If they do, it will likely be at dawn. It's best we not be around then."

Some miles ahead Gus Grissom and his men heard distant gunfire. They halted their horses, looking back. Paco Lopez trotted to the top of the nearest rise.

"See anything?" Gus called.

Paco shook his head.

"What do you think it is, Gus?" asked Virge Harper.

"Don't know," said Gus.

"Could it be some of that posse got through, and they're still following us?"

"Maybe, but I don't think so. If there was any survivors, seems they'd have run for San Miguel. And from the sound of that gunfire we heard earlier, there wasn't no survivors."

"Then it's somebody else," said Cherokee

Bill. "Either somebody who just happens to be out here—a prospector, maybe—or it's somebody else who's following us."

"Who the hell could that be?" said Gus, as much to himself as to the rest of his men, and there was a note of worry in his voice.

Paco was back now. The four bandits looked at one another. Beth McNally sat her horse quietly, seemingly beyond caring what happened to her.

Gus recovered his confidence. "Well, if it's somebody else following us, he's got hisself one big set of *cojones*."

"Like me," bragged Virge, and he turned to the McNally woman. "Right, ma'am?"

Beth said nothing, and Virge laughed.

Gus was getting more and more irritated with Virge. "Is that all you think about? I swear, you got your brain between your legs. Come on, let's get out of here."

CHAPTER 10

CAROLYN WAS TORN AND BLOODIED BY cactus, her red hair matted with sweat. More blood trickled down her right shoulder where it had been creased by the Apache bullet.

"Let me put a bandage on that," Sam told her.

She shook him off. "No. It's nothing."

They unsaddled the horses, which were beat down and lathered with sweat, especially Carolyn's sorrel blaze. Sam's coyote dun would be all right after a good blow. They rubbed down the animals with empty burlap sacks that Sam carried in his blanket roll, then watered them sparingly from their canteens. Afterward Sam explored the cave, hoping to find a water seep, but he found none.

"The water bags are gone with the packhorse," he told Carolyn when he came back. "We'll have to make do with what's in our canteens. How much have you got left?"

They each carried two canteens on their horses, which they had filled from the water bags that morning. Carolyn shook hers. "One full, one almost empty."

Sam nodded. "I'm about the same. We could probably dig for water in that dry wash, but the Apaches are there. We'll wait here till dark, then we'll leave."

"Are you sure we shouldn't stay?" asked Carolyn. "This looks like a good place to fight from."

"I'm not sure of anything," Sam told her. "But if they're of a mind, those Apach' could starve us out here. Or, they could wait for us to go crazy with thirst. *Or*, they could sneak up close and rush us at dawn. We got no backdoor out of here if things go bad."

"So where are we headed?"

"Away from here, as far and as fast as we can."

"Are you still going after Gus Grissom?"

Sam looked at her. "That's what I set out to do, Miss Manning. I don't leave a job unfinished."

They ate fried jerky and hardtack from Sam's saddlebags, and they considered themselves lucky to get that. With the packhorse gone, there was no grain for the horses, and there was no grazing for them around the cave. As it grew dark Sam and Carolyn wrapped the horses' hooves in strips cut from their spare clothes, to muffle sound on the rocks. They made sure their weapons were loaded and everything on their saddles tied down securely. They stoked their small fire, hoping to make the Indians think they were still at the cave.

The purple dusk dropped from the sky with desert swiftness. Soon it was pitch dark. "Now," Sam said, "before the moon comes up."

They stood. Each took a swallow of water. They loosened weapons in holsters and scabbards and peered into the darkness, wondering what lay out there.

"Scared?" Sam asked Carolyn.

"Of course I am," she told him. "But not scared enough to keep me from doing what I came here to do."

Sam shook his head. "You're one determined lady."

"Precisely," she said. Then she added, "Besides, there's not much risk, at least right now, is there? I understand Indians don't fight at night."

"They don't *like* to fight at night, but it doesn't mean they won't. If they catch us sneaking past them, they'll be more than happy to give us a scrap."

"Oh," Carolyn said.

Sam waved her forward. "Keep close. Lose me in the dark, and we may not hook up again."

"Yesterday that's what you wanted."

"Things have changed since yesterday."

"You mean, you may actually need me?"

"I wouldn't go quite that far."

They started down the shale slope in front of

the cave. Their footsteps and those of the horses seemed unnaturally loud in the darkness. They pinched the horses' nostrils, to quiet them. Sam's heart was thumping so loudly in his chest, he thought the Apaches would hear it. He expected at any second to see forms rising from the earth around them. He hoped that the Apache plan was to hide in the wash and creep forward later, when they expected the whites to be asleep. With luck the Indians would remain all night just outside the cave, then rush in at dawn—to find Sam and Carolyn gone.

And then what would they do? There was no telling. They might . . .

There was a noise, off to the right. Sam stopped, motioning Carolyn to do the same. They waited, but heard nothing more. Sam waved Carolyn on again.

The quarter moon rose. Its thin, silvery light gave faint illumination. Sam and Carolyn seemed to be all alone on the desert, but Sam knew from experience that looks could be deceiving. He guided them south and east, roughly toward the next pass through the mountains that would lead them to Arispe. After several hours of walking they stopped for a break.

"So far so good," Sam said in a low voice.

"Do you think they'll follow us?" Carolyn asked.

"Depends. They're on a murder raid. They might feel they've killed enough to satisfy their honor without looking for more trouble. On the other hand, they might decide they need to take revenge for the one we killed in front of the cave."

They unwrapped their horses' hooves, then they mounted and kept going. They rode the rest of the night and through the dawn. Carolyn slumped in the saddle, trying to keep her eyes open. The Spanish-style hat hung behind her head by its chin strap; her hair was in disarray. She was saddle sore and footsore, worn down from fear and exhaustion.

Overhead, the stars faded. The black sky turned gray. At last the sun rose above the eastern hills, throwing its already harsh light across the desert.

"This country look any different to you than it did a few minutes ago?" Sam asked after a bit.

Carolyn looked around, thinking this was some kind of trick question. "No," she said. "Should it?"

"According to my calculations, we're in Mexico now."

Carolyn was too tired to be impressed. "Where are the brass bands?"

"They must be late sleepers."

They kept going till past midmorning, when they stopped and rested in the shade of a rock overhang. Carolyn uncorked her canteen and raised it to her parched lips.

Sam took the canteen away. "Save it for the horses," he told her.

"What about us?" Carolyn protested.

"If we don't keep these horses going, it won't make much difference about us. They're wore down enough now from lack of grain."

Carolyn's face fell. "What are we supposed to drink? Is there any water in this country?"

Sam pointed to a distant line of mountains rising from the plain. "Nearest spring's in a place called Antelope Canyon."

To Carolyn the mountains looked a long way off. "Can we get there before these canteens run out?"

Sam was doubtful. "We'll try, but it's going to be tight."

Carolyn took a deep breath, steeling herself for the ordeal. "Oh, well. Mother said I'd lead an interesting life."

They made themselves as comfortable as possible and dozed in the shade of the overhang until the intensity of the sun's rays diminished. Then they rode on, moving at the plodding pace of their tired, thirsty horses. It was too hot for talk; and anyway, talk would only make them thirstier.

In the late afternoon they made camp. They were on an open, sandy plain. The cactus was largely gone; the main vegetation was scattered brush. They let the horses graze on what little grass they could find, then staked and cross-hobbled them. "No fire tonight," Sam informed Carolyn as they rolled out their blankets. He offered her some of the jerky and bread.

"No, thank you," she told him dispiritedly.

"You should eat," he said.

She shook her head. "Eating that salty meat and biscuit will just make me thirstier than I already am."

Sam ate, then washed it down with a sip of water. Carolyn took a drink from her canteen as well. Carolyn was half-faint from exhaustion, but she took her knife and drew another line down the center of the camp.

"You never give up, do you?" Sam marveled.

"I believe in making sure we know where we stand with one another. In my experience men are all alike."

Sam raised an amused eyebrow. "How much experience do you have?"

Her tone grew frosty. "I don't discuss my personal life, Mr. Slater."

"Yes, ma'am," Sam said, grinning. "I mean, no ma'am." He took up his rifle. "I'll stand first guard."

Carolyn started to lie down, then stopped. "The last time you said that, you sneaked out on me in the middle of the night."

"I wish you'd stop reminding me about that. I told you, things have changed."

Sam settled into his position while it was still light. Slowly, methodically, he memorized the location of every stand of brush within fifty yards of the camp. He had deliberately picked a camp spot with an open field of fire. Behind him the horses shuffled in their hobbles. Carolyn drew her blankets around herself and rested her head on the saddle. "Good night, Mr. Slater."

"Good night, Miss Manning. We'll need to be quiet tonight. I hope you don't snore."

"And if I do? Are you going to hit me over the head to silence me?"

"Probably," Sam told her. Christ, but he would hate to be married to that one.

Carolyn fell asleep instantly. It was soon dark. Sam watched the ground around him, rifle cradled in his arms. His nerves were keyed up, but not enough to dispel the weariness brought on by the events of the day. His body wanted to go limp, to relax. He fought to ward off sleep.

He tried to concentrate on the brush, but he found his mind wandering. How long before he could call on Carolyn to take over so he could get some sleep? But could he trust Carolyn to stand guard? Would she be able to spot Apaches closing in—if, which he doubted, there were any Apaches out there? Or would he have to stay awake all night, and the night after. . . .

He shook his head and blinked his eyes rapidly. He had almost dozed off. He shifted slightly, to get the blood flowing through his body. He opened his eyes wide and tried to hold them like that. Nothing around him had changed. There was nothing but the breeze and the eternal howl of coyotes, the poor man's orchestra. Nothing had changed at all. . . .

His head bobbed onto his chin. He shook it again. He could feel his eyes closing, and he shook his head once more. He took a deep breath and forced himself to concentrate on the singing of the coyotes. He blinked very slowly; the motion seemed to last a long time. He blinked again. He felt his head nodding. . . .

HE AWOKE WITH A START. HIS MOUTH WAS dry, his eyes crusted. He had no idea how long he'd been out. He swallowed, trying to work up some saliva, and looked at the Dipper. Christ, he'd been asleep for hours. The short summer night was nearly over. He looked around. Carolyn was still asleep; the horses were quiet as well.

Sam's eyes moved slowly from left to right, checking the camp's perimeter. He wiped the back of his mouth with a trembling hand as he realized that he could have been killed while he slept.

All those stories about him being impossible

to kill—they sounded good, and the legend sometimes gave him an edge in a fight, but no man was impossible to kill. All it took was one slip, one bit of bad luck, one time falling asleep when he should have been on . . .

His eyes stopped. He stared. That clump of brush maybe thirty yards away—it was hard to tell the distance in the dark—he could have sworn it hadn't been there before.

He went cold inside; his stomach twisted taut. He was imagining things, he had to be. There had been no sign that they'd been followed.

He let his eyes circle the camp perimeter once more, then came back to the questionable clump of brush. He could have sworn that it had grown slightly larger. He fixed its position against the background of stars and watched. Yes, it moved—ever so slightly, but it moved. This time there was no doubt.

Silently Sam thumbed back his rifle's hammer. He was going to feel like the world's biggest fool if he was wrong. More important, he was about to give away his and Carolyn's position to anyone who wanted to know where they were.

He checked the brush's position against the stars once again. He was sure that he was right now. He aimed the rifle, drew his breath, and squeezed the trigger.

There was a flash and a bang, and in front of him a yell of pain split the night. He heard Carolyn awaken. Even as she did, the ground before him seemed to come alive as shadowy figures ran forward, yelling and firing rifles and pistols.

Sam stood and fired back, levering off shells faster than he would have liked, not aiming. He heard Carolyn open up with her carbine, and he thought to himself that now they would find out how good she was.

Muzzle flashes sparkled in the darkness; the hammering of gunfire filled Sam's ears. Bullets zipped around Sam and Carolyn. From seemingly out of nowhere an Apache ran up to Sam with a clump of rabbitbrush tied to his headband. Sam swung his heated rifle barrel, caught the Indian across the throat, and leveled him.

Then Sam was hit by a driving force in the gut and knocked to the ground, dropping his rifle. He lay stunned, trying to suck air from the blow to the gut and regain his senses enough to fight back. He heard gunfire around him but had no idea what was happening. The Indian was covered with grease to prevent an enemy from getting a good hold on him. He leaped on Sam, pinning Sam's left arm with his right knee and Sam's right arm with his left wrist. In the Indian's right hand was a stone war club. He raised the club and swung it downward. Sam swerved his head just enough to make the weapon miss. He heard the stone head crunch the gravel beside him; he felt it whisper through the ends of his hair. Before the Indian could raise the club again, Sam leaned his head over and sank his teeth into the Indian's hand.

The Indian grunted with surprise and pain. He tried to withdraw his hand. Sam hung on with the tenacity of a rabid bulldog, working his teeth into the soft fleshy area between the thumb and the rest of the hand, grinding and chewing. The Indian tried to pull free with all his strength. It felt like Sam's teeth were being ripped out of his head, but he didn't let go. To let go meant death. He concentrated his whole being on what he was doing. Blood squirted into his mouth. There was the taste of dirt and grease. The Apache cursed and grunted.

The two men squirmed around, locked in an embrace of death. The back of Sam's shirt was torn by rocks. Somewhere there was gunfire and yelling. Sam kept working his teeth; he felt them dig into bone. Above him there was a sharp intake of breath.

Then the Indian could stand the pain no more. He released Sam's wrist with his left hand and took the war club from his imprisoned right. Sam took advantage of the break. As the Indian raised the club for the killing blow, Sam drew his pistol from its holster, jammed the barrel against the Indian's rib, and fired.

The Indian groaned and shuddered. He swayed, then flopped over, his legs across Sam's chest.

Sam lay there, chest heaving, trying to catch his breath. He could still taste the dead Indian's blood in his mouth. He closed his eyes, then opened them again, trying to rouse himself to action.

He turned and saw Carolyn Manning standing nearby, holding her carbine and watching with seeming unconcern. "Why—why didn't you help me?" he asked her.

"You looked like you were doing all right," she said.

Sam rolled the dead Apache off of him and stood. His limbs felt like they had been drained of their strength. "Where are the rest of them?" he asked Carolyn.

"Gone."

Sam's teeth hurt. His arms hurt where the Indian had pinned him. The rear of his head was grazed where the Indian's club had just missed, and his back was torn and scratched from rocks. Impossible to kill? he thought. Another inch and his skull would have been turned to porridge.

There was no sign of the Apaches. The one he had just killed lay at his feet. The one he had clubbed and the rest of the casualties—if any—had been carried off. A splash of blood on the ground told him that at least one more had been hit.

Then Sam realized that something else was gone, too. "Our horses. They got the horses."

"Yes," said Carolyn. "I tried to stop them, but I couldn't, not by myself."

"You act like I invited that fellow to jump me," Sam swore. Then he squatted, letting his head clear, sifting dirt through his fingers. "There's no turning back, we'd have too far to go. We'll either make Antelope Canyon on foot, or . . . or we won't."

Carolyn nodded solemnly. Sam had to admit that she had a knack for taking bad news well.

There was a distant yell.

Sam stood, looking. Gray dawn streaked the eastern sky. Outlined against it an Apache stood on a low swell, about three hundred yards off. The Apache was tall, with an air of authority, and Sam realized that it must be Chiquito. As Sam and Carolyn watched, the Apache bent over, presenting his backside to them. He flipped up his breechclout and began enthusiastically thumping his buttocks.

It was the lowest form of Apache insult. Sam swore under his breath. He grabbed Carolyn's carbine, cocking it. The carbine would just about make that range. Sam aimed and fired.

Chiquito leaped into the air, howling, and ran off in the dim light.

Sam handed the carbine back to Carolyn. "That makes three of us that won't be riding for a while," he said.

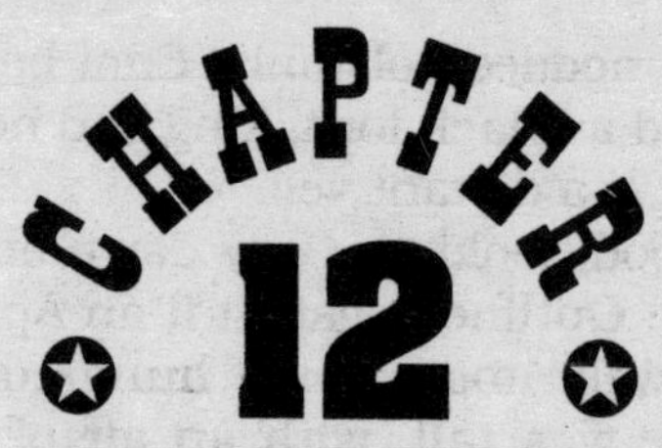

CHAPTER 12

BETH MCNALLY LAY ON HER SIDE IN THE darkness, chewing the rope that bound her wrist to that of the man called Gus. Gus kept her tied to him so that she wouldn't try to escape—also so that she'd be handy in case he felt the need for her during the night. He was a heavy sleeper, and right now he was snoring, content. Beth smelled his rank breath and sweat, and the smell made her sick.

Beth didn't know where she'd go when she escaped, and she didn't care. She didn't care about food or water, either. She didn't really care if she died. Anything was better than this—and the fate that Gus had planned for her.

She worked carefully, quietly, trying not to

wake Gus, but the rope was strong, and she was frustrated because she was making so little progress. She had to get it done before dawn, because if she didn't, Gus would see what she had been up to, and she would be in for another beating. She still ached from the first beating, and the ones that had come after.

"Pssst."

Beth turned her head. In the faint moonlight she saw the skinny blond called Virge, who was standing guard.

Beth's heart leaped, in a cold, calculating way. Here was her chance. All afternoon, since Virge and Gus had had the argument over her, she had been covertly making eyes at Virge, smiling at him, hoping to lure him into doing something foolish. Then she grew worried. What if he had seen what she was up to, and he was going to wake Gus . . . ?

"Pssst." Virge beckoned to her. Of all the bandits Virge was the worst. His physical demands were insatiable. He never got enough. Since their argument Gus had made Virge stay away from Beth, and the ex-cowboy had been pining like a child without its new toy. She had been offered to Paco and the brooding Cherokee Bill, but they had refused—either because they weren't interested or because they didn't want to offend Gus.

Virge came closer, grinning. He had managed to convince himself that Beth actually liked him, certainly that she preferred him to Gus. Beth didn't know whether it was youthful delusion, stupidity, or a combination of the two, but right now she was glad of it.

Virge squatted beside her, looking around to make sure no one was watching. "Want to come with me?" he whispered.

Beth smiled at him. Then, ruefully, she held up her wrist, showing the rope that bound her to Gus.

Virge drew his knife and began cutting the rope. He never even noticed where she had been gnawing at it. He knew there would be trouble with Gus later, but he was so infatuated with Beth that he didn't care. As he worked he kissed her swollen, sun-blackened lips. She forced herself to ignore the pain and kiss him back. It was the hardest thing she'd ever done in her life.

"Hurry," she whispered as Gus snorted and rolled over in his blankets.

Virge finished with the rope. He took up the slack and laid the broken end down gently, careful not to disturb Gus. He helped Beth up and led her away from the camp, down a draw, where they wouldn't be heard.

"Aren't you worried about Gus?" she said, squeezing his hand.

"Shee-it, I ain't scart of Gus. Way I handle a gun, I ain't scart of no man."

Beth pretended to stumble and went to one knee. She felt around in the dark and palmed a large rock as Virge pulled her back to her feet. Virge was far enough away from camp now. He could no longer control himself. He drew Beth to him and began kissing her roughly, pawing her breasts and buttocks.

"Come on now. Come on, woman," he moaned. He fumbled with the buttons on what was left of her blouse and tried to drag her to the ground at the same time. As he did so Beth raised the rock and brought it down on his skull.

"Ow!" he cried.

He grabbed his head and stepped away. Beth raised the rock and hit him again, as hard as she could, almost knocking herself down.

Virge grunted and fell to the ground. Beth wondered if she had killed him and hoped that she had. She reached down and took the knife from his belt. She wanted his pistol, too, but he groaned and moved, and she got scared. She got up and ran back down the draw toward the camp.

She reached the camp and went to the picketed horses. Somebody else was awake now; she heard sleepy mumblings. Trying to keep calm, she hacked through the horses' picket lines, leaving her own mount for last. She waved the freed horses out of the camp.

"Go on! Shoo! Shoo!"

All the bandits were awake now. There were footsteps behind Beth as she grabbed her horse's mane and awkwardly climbed onto the animal, bareback. A hand reached for her and she kicked it away. The horse reared, knocking somebody backward. The figure uttered a surprised oath, then Beth kicked the horse in the ribs and galloped out of camp.

* * *

Behind Beth the bandits were yelling and cursing. Cherokee Bill raised a pistol to shoot her, but Gus pulled his arm down.

"I want her alive," Gus said. He looked at the severed wrist rope. "How'd she get away? Where's Virge at?"

Virge stumbled up, holding his head. The other men could see blood trickling down his neck.

"What happened?" Gus demanded.

"I don't know," Virge replied. "She snuck up and hit me with something. A rock, it must have been."

"This rope is cut. Where'd she get a knife at?"

"Damn if I know."

Gus stared at Virge for a second, then turned to the others. "Get the horses. Saddle up."

Cherokee Bill said, "Let her go, Gus. She ain't worth it."

"He's right," Paco joined in. The Mexican's unbound hair hung in a thick mass around his shoulders. "It is unsafe for us here with the Apache around. We must get to Arispe."

"We will," Gus said. "But not till we catch that McNally bitch. I ain't done with her."

"Me neither," Virge said.

Bill and Paco looked dismayed. "Don't just stand around," Gus barked. "Let's get them horses."

Beth couldn't tell where she was going in the dark; she couldn't read the stars. Her parents could have read them, but she couldn't. She just rode, letting her horse pick the way. She was not used to riding bareback, and it was a struggle to remain on the horse. Her legs and back ached. Her rear and thighs were rubbed raw and bleeding from two days in the saddle, and each movement of the horse brought white-hot pain to them, but she gritted her teeth and kept going, even as the tears rolled down her cheeks.

She was tired and sleepy, arm weary from gripping the horse's mane. Then the horse spooked at something in the darkness—she never knew what. The animal reared, and Beth lost her grip first on the horse's chest with her legs, then on its mane, and she fell off. The horse galloped away, leaving her on foot.

There was no chance of recapturing the horse in the dark, so Beth started walking. Maybe it would work out for the best, she told herself. Maybe the bandits would follow the horse and not her—for she was certain that the bandits would come after her. Paco and the mean-looking one called Bill wouldn't care, but Gus and Virge would want her back.

Dawn broke, and Beth realized she was heading toward the mountains, in almost the same direction the bandits had been taking her. She thought about turning back for San Miguel, but she knew she could never make the trek in her battered condition, with no food or water. Also, there was no place to hide on the plain. If she kept going this way, she might come upon a village and get help. It was either that, or die. But if she had to die, at least she would be free.

Beth was from the small town of Los Angeles, California. Her parents had been forty-niners, come west on the Overland Trail. They hadn't found gold, but her father had founded a prosperous hardware business and later moved south because he preferred the warmer climate. They had raised Beth in the solid, middle-class fashion that they themselves had known back in Ohio. They had wanted her to go away to college and become a teacher, but she had met Jim McNally, a young Arizonan with big ambitions. She had fallen head over heels in love with Jim. Against her parents' wishes the two of them had gotten married, and she had followed Jim to the arid southwest, to raise cattle.

Beth had been willing to endure Arizona's hardships—her parents had endured at least as much in their early days in California. Jim had been her whole life. They had planned a future together, and now . . .

Now she didn't know. She was just motivated by the instinct to survive.

She continued on, exhausted. The sun rose higher, and a dust cloud in the west told her the bandits were coming. Beth fled deeper into the hills, to hide. She turned down a narrow canyon, doing what she thought was a good job of concealing her footprints. When she reached a spot where she had a view back up the canyon, she crouched among the rocks and brush. She breathed easy, thinking she was safe. Then she saw Paco and Cherokee Bill coming. They leaned over in their saddles, somehow following her tracks. Gus and Virge must be right behind them.

Beth left the rocks and went deeper into the canyon, only to find that there was no way out. It was what Jim used to call a box canyon. She looked over her shoulder. Paco and Cherokee Bill were closing in. She couldn't go back that way. She had no choice but to climb.

Up the rocks she went. Behind her there were cries. The bandits had seen her. She moved as fast as she could. It was a steep, dangerous climb. Sweat poured off her, making her skinned thighs burn so badly that she wanted to cry out.

Below her, Beth heard the bandits ride to the foot of the canyon wall. They shouted, but she kept climbing, not looking back. At least they didn't shoot at her. Her arms and legs ached, her thighs felt like they were going to split, but she wasn't going to stop while there was any hope at all. She would rather fall and be smashed to death on the rocks than be back in their hands.

Near the top the rock was smooth. Beth hauled herself painfully upward, seeking handholds and footholds, breaking her fingernails, cutting her knees, knowing that if she slipped and fell she would die. Paco and Cherokee Bill watched, fascinated, as she made her way up. They didn't come after. The climb was too dangerous.

At last she reached the top. She pulled herself over, feet scrabbling on the rock's smooth surface. She lay on her stomach, breathless, all in, her face against the rough rock. She felt fresh blood oozing from her cracked lips. After a bit she raised herself up—to see Gus sitting not twenty yards away, watching her. Virge stood behind him, looking worried.

Gus touched his hat brim and gave her that big smile. The smile was attractive in a cruel way, and Beth imagined that a certain kind of woman would find him desirable. "Morning," he said.

Beth lay back down. There were no tears, no curses. She had nothing left to give. She thought of throwing herself off the cliff wall, but she no longer had the energy for that, either, or the will.

Gus stood and reached her with one stride. The smile faded as he grabbed her arm and jerked her to her feet. "Get up, bitch."

Beth stood without emotion. Gus reached back and slapped her already swollen cheek. She barely flinched.

"You gave us a real rough morning, looking for our horses," Gus told her. "Wasn't a nice thing to do. By the way, we found your horse a ways back. No need to thank us, we're just happy-go-lucky gentlemen, always looking to do a lady a good turn. It's lucky we caught up to you, you know. You might have done yourself some harm."

He slapped her again, this time knocking her a few steps backward, and his dark eyes flashed with anger. "How'd you do it? How'd you get away?"

Beth nodded toward Virge. "Why don't you ask him?"

Gus turned. "What's she saying, Virge?"

Virge tried to make light of it. "Shee-it, she's just looking for a way out of—"

"Ask him who cut the rope," Beth said.

Gus turned away from Beth. His eyes were narrow now, shrewd, his face full of grim satisfaction. "I knew it," he told Virge. "I knew it was you."

"All right, so what if it was?" Virge burst out. "I got a right to her, ever' bit as much as you. You can't go around telling me what—"

Gus smashed Virge's jaw with an overhand right. The blow sent Virge reeling backward. Gus followed him, pounding him with a left, then another right, knocking him on the seat of his pants.

Virge shook the cobwebs from his head. He spat blood. He got up and launched himself at Gus's gut. Gus sidestepped Virge's wild charge, clubbing him behind the ear, knocking him onto his chest just inches from the edge of the cliff. Before Virge could recover, Gus hauled him up, turned him, and hit him flush on the cheek, knocking him down once more.

Angrily Virge reached for his pistol, but Gus drew his weapon first, cocking it.

"It's your call, Virge," Gus said.

Virge looked at him, breathing heavily. Blood trickled from his lip; his jaw was already swelling. Then he pushed the pistol back into its holster.

"I'm ramrodding this outfit," Gus told him, "and don't you forget it. You'll get this bitch when and if I say so. *Comprende, amigo?*"

Virge didn't answer.

"*Comprende?*" Gus repeated, pointing the pistol.

Virge let out his breath. "*Comprende*," he muttered.

Gus holstered his pistol and turned back to Beth, who stood looking defiant. He grabbed her long hair and twisted it around his fist, making her bend over, grimacing with pain. "And you. You go trying to split up this outfit again, and I swear to God I'll let the Mexicans mate you with their donkeys when we get to Arispe. And if they don't do it, I will. You got that?"

Lips drawn back with pain, Beth nodded.

Gus gave her a shove, pushing her away. Then he got a canteen from his saddle and tossed it to her, and his old smile came back. "Have a drink. We don't want you dyin' on us now, do we? That'd take all the fun out of this little trip. Besides, you're worth too much."

Gus turned to Virge. "Get up, and let's go. We wasted too much time as it is. We're just lucky that posse ain't after us no more."

Virge stood, rubbing his sore jaw. He spat more blood. "What about them other fellas that was chasin' us?"

For a moment Gus looked worried, as if he saw something that was invisible to everyone else. Then he shook it off and said, "Whoever they were, the Apaches got them, too."

"You sure?"

"I'm sure. If they got the posse, they got them, too. They had to."

AS THE SUN ROSE SAM AND CAROLYN PREpared to leave their little camp. "No sense wasting time," Sam said.

"What about the Apaches?" Carolyn asked.

Sam shrugged. "They got our horses. Maybe that'll be enough for them. If it's not, there's not much we can do about it. We can't stay here, not with our water the way it is. We have to get to Antelope Canyon. We couldn't have picked a worse spot to be thirsty. Most places we could dig for it or chop cactus. Here, there's nothing."

"Are you sure there's water in Antelope Canyon?" Carolyn asked him.

"I told you before, I'm not sure of anything."

"And Gus Grissom, what about him?"

"Grissom is miles ahead of us by now. The Apaches chased us in the other direction from the one Grissom was traveling, and he has horses, besides."

"Can we still catch them before they reach Arispe?"

Sam marveled at her sense of purpose. "Catching them's the last thing on my mind just now, lady. I'm more concerned with staying alive. It would take a miracle for us to keep them from getting to Arispe."

"Don't you believe in miracles?"

"I haven't seen many lately."

They stared across the lightening plain, toward the distant mountains, where the water lay. "It's going to be a difficult walk," Carolyn said.

"Talking about it won't make it any easier. If you got any excess baggage, get rid of it now."

They abandoned their saddles, bridles, and blankets at the campsite. They left their coats and spare clothes. Carolyn left her saddlebags as well.

"What about that money you're carrying?" Sam asked her.

Carolyn tapped her waistband. "I have it in a money belt."

Sam packed some food and ammunition in his saddlebags, leaving everything else behind. He cut a length of rope and made a sling for

Carolyn's carbine, and she slung the weapon over her shoulder. They finished the little bit of water that remained in their first canteens. Carolyn started to toss the empty canteen away.

"Save it," Sam told her. "You'll need it when we get to water."

Sam picked up his rifle and draped the saddlebags over his shoulder. "Ready?" he said.

Carolyn nodded.

"Let's go, then."

They started off, their shadows thrown long across the plain by the newly risen sun. They trudged along quietly. As the sun rose higher the heat welled up in shimmering waves from the sandy soil. There was no ignoring it, and with the heat came growing thirst. Sam picked up a handful of pebbles and gave some to Carolyn.

"Suck on these. It'll help ease the thirst."

"A large pitcher of lemonade would help more," Carolyn commented.

Sam was used to walking long distances; his high-topped Apache moccasins were made for it. Carolyn hobbled behind him, in riding boots that were nearly new. The soles were thin and the leather pinched her feet. The boots had raised blisters earlier, during the stretches when she and Sam had been forced to walk. Now the blisters swelled and broke, and the exposed inner skin was rubbed raw and bleeding. Carolyn felt blood squishing around inside the boots. It became agony for her to walk, and she started falling further and further behind Sam.

Sam stopped and came back to her. "Sit down," he said.

Gingerly she lowered herself to the ground. Her feet and legs were swollen so badly that Sam had to slit her boots with his knife and pull them off. He removed his flannel shirt, leaving only his wool undershirt to protect him from the sun. "I ought to clean these," he said, examining her bloody feet, "but we can't spare any water." While Carolyn leaned back on her hands, eyes partly closed against the pain, Sam cut his dirty shirt into strips and gently wrapped the strips around her feet.

"You have a tender side, Mr. Slater," Carolyn observed.

Sam grinned through two weeks' growth of beard—he'd never had time to get cleaned up in San Miguel. "Don't let it get around. Might ruin my reputation."

"Your reputation means a lot to you, doesn't it? You wouldn't want people to think you're actually human."

Sam didn't rise to the bait. "My reputation is just another weapon. I like to keep it sharp."

When he was finished, he said, "All done. Have a drink, and let's go."

She took her canteen and uncorked it. She raised it to her lips, then stopped. "Aren't you having any?"

"No."

"Then neither am I," she said, and she recorked the canteen.

Sam helped her stand, and they started off once more. Just before noon they laid up, in the lee of a small rise. With his knife Sam scooped a depression in the base of the rise. Then he cut some brush and built an awning for his improvised dugout. The dugout was just big enough for the two of them to sit in and be shaded from the sun.

"It ain't much, but it'll help," he said as they squeezed under.

"Did you learn this from the Apaches?" Carolyn said.

"Just common sense."

They sat side by side under the brush awning, their shoulders touching. "Did you like living with the Apaches?" Carolyn asked Sam.

Sam was quiet for a moment, then he said, "Yes. Not at first, but after I'd been with them awhile. They had a very . . . natural way of life. Nothing artificial. You felt at one with the world around you, part of a greater whole—I don't know, it's hard to describe, but it was almost a mystical feeling. You were part of nature, not separate from it. It's a good way to live—or it was, before the white men came and destroyed it."

"What are they like—the Apaches, I mean?"

"Proud, honest, loyal, funny."

"Funny? I never thought of Indians as having a sense of humor."

"That's cause you've never known any. There's nothing Apaches like better than a good laugh." He thought a moment. "I guess what they do best is endure. An Apache can endure just about anything—except civilization."

When the sun's rays had lessened, Sam and Carolyn left the little dugout. They walked the rest of the afternoon and into the night. Though they drank sparingly from their canteens, the levels inside went inexorably down, until both Sam and Carolyn were reduced to a few drops of brackish liquid. And still their thirst raged. For a camp that night they simply lay down where they stopped. They were too tired to stand guard. If the Apaches came for them, so be it. The temperature fell, and sometime during the night Sam and Carolyn huddled together for warmth, hardly aware that they were doing it.

Sam had Carolyn up and on the march again before dawn, taking advantage of the early-morning coolness. Somewhere an owl hooted on its last pass of the night. The faint smell of sage tinted the air. Then the sun rose, a red ball in the eastern sky, a sign of the heat to come. Carolyn unstopped her canteen and tilted it to her lips, but it was empty.

"Here," Sam said, passing her his.

"I can't," she protested. "This is all you—"

"Take it. I'm used to this." He spoke slowly,

his words sounding funny because his tongue was beginning to swell.

They slogged along. The sun rose further, and the full force of the heat blasted them. They had stopped sweating; there was not enough water for sweat in their salt-encrusted bodies. At one point Carolyn unslung the carbine from her shoulder and let it fall to the ground. She kept going without a backward look at it.

They were down to the contents of one canteen, and at the midday break they each drank from it. "That's the end," Sam said, tapping the hollow-sounding canteen.

They exchanged looks. "We're not going to make it, are we?" Carolyn said. She was as cool as always, the only difference being a hint of resignation in her voice.

"There's always a chance," Sam replied.

They started off again. It was hard to breathe with swollen throats and tongues. The little moisture left in their bodies was sucked out of them by the ovenlike heat.

"I don't suppose there's any chance of a thunderstorm?" Carolyn muttered.

Sam looked at the cloudless sky. "About as much as there is of snow."

"I was afraid you'd say that."

They staggered along, the sandy soil pulling at their feet. Once again Carolyn fell behind Sam. Blood soaked through the improvised bandages on her feet. Then she swooned and fell. She tried to get up, making it to her hands and knees. Sam came back for her. He helped her to her feet, and they kept on.

For Carolyn, the day seemed to have no end. The sun seemed to burn itself into her brain. Then the sun started spinning, and she thought that was odd. The entire sky seemed to be spinning now, the whole world. Everything was going faster, faster. . . .

Sam heard a moan, followed by a thud.

Slowly he turned. Carolyn had collapsed. Sam went back. He knelt, resting her head in his lap and fanning her with his hat. "Miss Manning? Carolyn?"

Her eyes fluttered but did not open. She made faint moaning sounds.

Sam looked toward the mountains, his throat raw from thirst. For a split second he almost panicked. He wanted to get up and start running for the mountains, for the water. Then he got hold of himself. It would be another day's walk to Antelope Canyon. He could make it by himself, maybe. But to do that he would have to leave Carolyn here. He would have to leave her to die.

He swore softly. He slung his rifle across his back. Then he got to his knees, lifted Carolyn in his arms, and stood.

He started walking, eyes fixed on the distant purple line of the mountains. He put all thoughts from his mind—the heat, the thirst, Carolyn's weight in his arms. He tried to become a machine, repetitive, without feeling. One step after another, he told himself. One step after another, that's all it took. If he could just keep putting one foot in front of the other, eventually he'd make Antelope Canyon. Eventually he'd reach water.

And what then?

Don't think about that. Don't think about anything.

He hadn't realized how uneven the ground was until he tried to carry someone across it. He labored up the slightest of rises and eased down the far sides, shifting his weight to the rear so he wouldn't fall. Carolyn's weight seemed to grow in his arms, until she felt like an armload of lead. His muscles were on fire with the effort of carrying her.

His steps grew unsteady, irregular. He was losing the battle. He gritted his teeth and tried harder. He shifted the unconscious woman in his arms, briefly easing the pain.

He staggered down an incline and lost his balance in the soft sand. He slipped, fell, and rolled to the bottom, dropping Carolyn, who rolled alongside him. Her eyes fluttered as she lay there, but it was the only sign of life.

Sam picked her up again and kept going. Step after step, yard after yard, mile after mile. His stride shortened, his steps faltered. At last he sank to the ground with his burden, unable to go further.

He lay there for he didn't know how long, with the sun hammering down on him. Then vibrations in the earth told him that horses were coming.

He raised himself to one elbow. Through swollen eyelids he saw riders approaching. They were Apaches, and in their lead was the war chief called Chiquito.

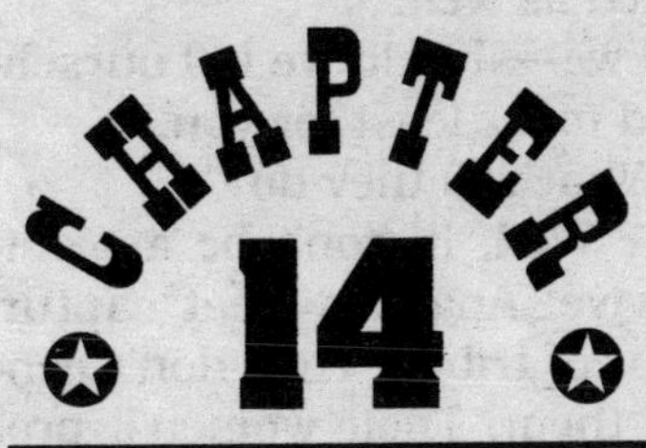

THE APACHES WERE BARE-CHESTED AND painted for war. The older ones, the warriors, circled Sam and Carolyn at a distance while two boys held Sam and Carolyn's horses, along with some other stolen horses, out of rifle range.

Next to Sam, Carolyn had regained consciousness. With difficulty she sat up, watching the Apaches, trying to focus her green eyes beneath the flat brim of the Spanish hat. "Aren't you going to shoot?" she asked Sam in a thirst-racked voice that did little to hide her fear.

Sam shook his head. "Wouldn't do any good. There's too many of them." Sam was going to die, anyway, but to start shooting now would get Carolyn killed as well.

"Should we—should we kill ourselves?"

"No need to, at least for you."

"Why? What will they do?"

"To you? Well, it won't be a picnic, but you should survive. Apaches treat captured women better'n a lot of tribes. They don't generally rape or mutilate them. Their women'll probably beat you and make you a slave around the camp, but eventually they'll sell you to the Mexicans or the army." He grinned. "Unless, of course, they fall for your winning personality and decide to punish one of their warriors by marrying you to him."

"I'm surprised you can maintain your sense of humor at a time like this, Mr. Slater. And what will happen to you?"

"Just hope you won't have to watch." Like as not they would tie him upside down over a slow fire, roasting him until his brains exploded out of his skull. His guts roiled with fear, fear that he fought hard not to show. He knew he should kill himself, but the Apache in him wouldn't let him take that step. He felt some perverse pride, some insane need to prove his manhood to these men.

As the circle around them contracted Sam and Carolyn stood. Sam held his Winchester low at his side, not threatening. Chiquito trotted forward, rifle butt propped on his naked thigh. His aquiline nose and handsome features denoted a strain of Mexican blood in his background, Sam thought. His coppery skin gleamed from the grease with which he had covered himself. Over his right shoulder was a three-strand medicine cord, tied at the left hip and decorated at intervals with shells and stones. As he drew closer Sam saw that he was sitting gingerly on piled blankets to ease the pain from the bullet that Sam had put in his rear.

Sam grinned as though he had no fear of these painted warriors, or of their leader. He spoke to Chiquito in Spanish. "Looks like you're having trouble riding."

Chiquito stiffened in his wicker saddle, and the movement caused him obvious pain. "The *inda* speaks boldly. Soon we will see how bold he is."

Still grinning, Sam indicated the two young apprentice warriors, who held the stolen horses. "That's a nice string of horses, *nantan*. You must be a mighty thief."

Now Chiquito smiled proudly. "We will fatten those animals on the long grasses of the Sierra Nevada, then sell them to the Mexicans for *aguardiente*."

Painfully Chiquito dismounted, followed by some of his men. One of the Apaches took Sam's rifle and pistol, and Sam made no attempt to stop him. To the Indians remaining on horseback, Chiquito said, "Find wood. Build a fire."

The bottom seemed to drop out of Sam's stomach, but he made himself stare into

Chiquito's dark eyes. The Apache war chief studied him, as if trying to read the mind of the man who dared to defy him this way. Then he saw the long scar beneath Sam's beard. He touched it. He examined Sam's Apache moccasins, and a look of understanding crossed his handsome face.

"You have a name among the *dine*," he suggested.

"That's right, *nantan*." Apaches never called one another by their names, except in the most unusual circumstances. Sam's Apache name to outsiders was Scar, but in the tribe he was called Tya-zali-ton, or "Sandy Whiskers."

Chiquito went on: "You were once one of the *dine*. I have heard of your father. He was a good man, a brave warrior."

"That is correct."

"Yet now you fight against the *dine*."

"The *dine* were trying to kill me, *nantan*. What would you have me do?"

Chiquito put his face close to Sam's. Sam could smell his rank breath as he spat out his words. "The white men have another name for you. They call you *Sla-ter-hay*."

It wasn't as bad as calling him by his Apache name. Still, the condescension was there. Not backing away from confrontation, Sam said, "You insult me, *nantan*. I have done nothing to earn this contempt. I could say that the Mexicans call you 'the little one,' *Chiquito-hay*."

Chiquito lost his temper. In one fluid motion he drew his knife and slashed at Sam, who skipped backward, barely avoiding the blade. Chiquito rushed in; Sam sidestepped and kicked him in the stomach. Chiquito fell, rolled, and jumped back to his feet before Sam could follow up his advantage.

Sam drew his own knife, which had not been taken away. He and Chiquito circled each other. The Apache chief's eyes gleamed with hatred of all white men.

Chiquito slashed. Sam parried and jumped back. He landed awkwardly, and because he was weak from thirst and fatigue, he slipped and fell. He caught himself on one hand as Chiquito leaped at him. Sam fell back and caught Chiquito's knife wrist with his left hand, at the same time the Apache caught Sam's knife wrist with his own free hand. Sam put a foot to the Apache's stomach and threw him over his head. Chiquito landed on his back, rolled, and came to his feet grabbing a handful of dirt, which he threw into Sam's face.

Sam had seen the move coming, but he was tired and his reflexes were slow. He was able to avoid some of the dirt but caught the rest in his eyes. Half-blinded, he backed up, slashing defensively. He was losing strength. He couldn't keep this up much longer. Chiquito drew back his knife and moved in for the kill.

At that moment Carolyn jumped between them. "Stop it! Stop it, you two!" she yelled, looking at both men in turn. "Are you both mad? Is killing each other the only thing you know how to do?"

Chiquito stayed the knife. He didn't understand all of Carolyn's words, but he understood her tone, and he admired her spirit. While Sam caught his breath Chiquito spoke to him. "The red-haired one is brave. She is your woman?"

Sam knew better than to lie. He shook his head. "She is not my woman."

"She is a relative, then—a sister?"

"No, she is not my sister, either."

Chiquito was surprised. "A friend?"

Sam and Carolyn looked at each other. Slowly Sam replied, "Yes, she is a friend."

"A good friend," Chiquito observed. As suddenly as it had erupted, his anger subsided, replaced by curiosity. "Why have you come to this place?"

Sam's throat was so raw from thirst that it hurt him to talk. "We are trailing a group of the *inda*. You have seen their tracks. They killed this woman's father and brother. If the Navajo kill the *nantan*'s family, does not the *nantan* pursue them until the wrong is made good?"

Chiquito nodded. "*Enjuh.* I understand revenge. I have spent much of my life seeking revenge. And you help this woman simply because she is your friend?"

Sam hesitated, afraid to tell the truth, that he was doing it for money. Fortunately Chiquito didn't wait for an answer. "To help a friend is good." He considered the situation for a moment, his face impassive. Then he glanced down at his bandaged rear. "Could you have killed me when you did this?"

"Yes, *nantan*, I could have."

Chiquito nodded and smiled, as if enjoying a joke on himself. He said something to his men, who laughed. One of them rode off to halt those who were gathering wood for the fire. Another returned Sam's rifle and pistol. While Sam holstered the pistol Chiquito walked back to his pony. From the saddle he removed a cow's intestine that had been filled with water and tied at both ends. He tossed the water skin to Sam, who caught it. "This is all the water we can spare. We also were going to follow the *inda*, but we will let you have them. Do you wish your horses back?"

Sam looked toward the mountains, calculating. "No. The horses will drink too much water. We will walk, and when this lady has taken revenge on her family's killers, we will take their horses."

Chiquito nodded again, sagely. "*Enjuh*. It is a good decision."

Chiquito slipped the three-strand medicine cord over his head. There was a cross at the end of it—Sam had often speculated that the decorated medicine cords were imitations of rosaries carried by the old Spanish missionaries—and Chiquito touched the cross to Sam's head. "This will prevent your steps from going astray on your journey. It will ensure that you find the men you are seeking."

Sam looked the Apache in the eye. "You have my thanks, *nantan*."

"Take care of the red-haired one," Chiquito said.

"I will."

"If it is Ussen's will, we shall meet again."

Sam nodded, then Chiquito turned away. With a shout to his men he vaulted onto his pony's back, and the Apaches rode off.

Sam and Carolyn watched the Indians go, then Sam turned to Carolyn. "I guess I owe you one."

"This time you didn't look like you were doing so well," she explained.

Carolyn and Sam sat down with the water skin. Carolyn's eyes widened as Sam untied one end. Her hands trembled. She could barely resist lunging for it. "Drink as much as you can," Sam said as he passed her the skin. "Better to have a lot at once than a little at different times."

They sated themselves with the water, taking care not to spill any, and they chewed a bit of jerky. Then Sam slung the water skin over his shoulder, and they started walking once more. They should have rested before starting off, but there was not enough water to allow that. Sam marveled at the way Carolyn hid the pain that her bandaged feet must be causing her. Sam's arms and thighs were sore from carrying her.

The mountains drew closer, but ever so slowly. They allowed themselves a campfire that night. They were too far behind the Grissom gang to be seen, and the Apaches were no longer interested in them.

As it grew dark they sat beside the fire, huddled against the growing cold, shivering and wishing they still had their blankets.

Carolyn said, "That was a smart move on your part back there—saying that we were friends."

"Seeing what we been through, it didn't seem all that much of an exaggeration," Sam told her. "Not anymore."

"I don't have many friends—many real friends, I mean."

"You got one now."

She looked at him, and in the dark her green eyes seemed to glow softly, like a cat's. "I appreciate that. I really do."

It was time to turn in, and Sam said, "Don't forget to draw your line."

Carolyn took her knife. Halfheartedly she started to draw a line in the dirt, not down the camp this time, but between where the two of them sat. Before it was complete, Sam slipped the knife from her hand.

She looked up at him. "No?"

"No," he said, and he took her in his arms and lowered his lips to hers.

Later Carolyn ran a fingernail down the long scar on Sam's cheek. "What was it like?" she breathed.

"Like tangling with a wildcat," Sam said.

She giggled and drew him to her again.

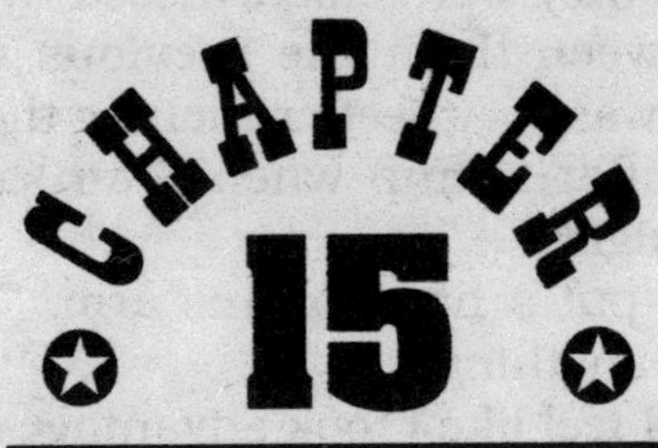

CHAPTER 15

SAM WOKE CAROLYN WELL BEFORE DAWN. "Time to go," he told her.

She stretched and looked up at him, her short red hair tousled, her green eyes strikingly warm. "I was hoping for another kind of wake-up service," she said.

Even after last night Sam was surprised by this boldness. "Later," he replied. "We got a lot of ground to cover today."

She sat up beside him, running a hand through his straw-colored hair and kissing his cheek. Then she gave his hand a squeeze and stood.

The two of them ate and drank some of their precious water, then started walking again. For a long while neither of them said anything. It was almost as if they were embarrassed by what had passed between them the previous night. The only sound was their feet crunching the sand.

It was after sunup when Sam said, "Look, about last night . . ."

Carolyn put a hand on his arm. "There's no need to say anything."

"I just—I feel like I took advantage of you."

"Don't. I wanted it to happen." She paused. "The only thing is, I don't know where this leaves us—after this is all over, I mean."

"We better wait and see if there *is* an after, 'fore we start making any plans," Sam said. Then he added, "I've got to tell you, Carolyn. I'm not a man for getting attached to one woman—or to any woman."

"You're a loner?"

"Some have called me that."

They walked on, and Carolyn said, "Maybe it's just as well. I don't know if I'm ready to fall for a man. I don't know if I could go through it again."

"You sound like you've been burned once," Sam said.

"I have been."

"Bad?"

She replied with surprising vehemence. "Very bad."

"Was this since you came to Texas?"

"Yes."

"I'm sorry."

"Why? It was no fault of yours."

"Prickly as ever, ain't you?" Sam said. "I've seen cactus it'd be easier to get close to."

She arched a playful eyebrow. "Or wildcats?"

Sam laughed. "Especially wildcats."

Carolyn grew serious once more. "What will we do after we get to Antelope Canyon?"

"There's villages south of there. We might be able to buy animals to ride in one of them."

"Horses?"

Sam shrugged. "In this country a mule's just as good."

That afternoon they reached the mountains. Once again they began the torturous routine of up-and-down climbing. The sun beat down, increasing their thirst. There were still a few drops left in the water skin when Sam stopped Carolyn.

"See that hawk?" he said, pointing to a reddish-brown bird, sailing through the air not far away. "That hawk never goes more than half a mile from water."

"You mean—Antelope Canyon?" she said. She felt like Moses speaking about the Promised Land.

"That's right."

They picked up their pace and soon entered a narrow canyon. Excited jays signaled the presence of the two intruders as they ascended the canyon. The source of the water was a subterranean stream that bubbled to the surface in the canyon bottom, flowed for a few hundred yards, then disappeared again into the sand. The stream was shaded by cottonwoods, willows, and a few sycamores, a startling sight in this land of rock and thorn. Black-and-yellow butterflies flitted through the lush grasses and wildflowers that grew along the stream's banks; insects hummed in tune to the gurgling water. The stream provided the life source for a variety of animals, whose tracks were to be seen all about.

Carolyn ran forward with a little cry. She lay down beside the stream and dunked her face in. After a moment she raised up again. The dirt on her face was streaked by the dripping water. "I'm sorry if I seem unladylike, but I never imagined plain water could be so inviting."

Sam squatted, dipping water with his hand and grinning at her. When the two of them had drunk their fill, Carolyn rolled on her back in the long grass. There were smooth boulders in the stream's middle and along its sides, and in these boulders were a great number of round, shallow holes.

"What are these?" Carolyn asked, standing and examining the curious holes more closely.

"They're *metates*," said Sam. "Grinding holes. Apache women use 'em to grind their corn."

"Is that how you knew about this canyon—from your time with the Apaches?"

"That's right. We used to camp here on trips in and out of Mexico."

Sam left Carolyn and explored the ground around the spring. "Grissom and his men have been here," he said on his return, "and not long ago."

"I thought you said they'd be far ahead of us by now?"

"Something's slowed them up. They came in from the wrong direction than they should have, so they must have gotten thrown off the trail, just like we did. It must have something to do with that woman they kidnapped. Maybe she got away and they went looking for her, or maybe they killed her and buried her where her body wouldn't be found. Whatever it was, it wasn't good."

The westering sun had long since left the canyon bottom in shadow. Sam looked around. "We might as well spend the night. We'll top off our canteens in the morning."

"We can camp right here," Carolyn said. "It's a lovely spot."

"No, we'll go up the canyon a ways. A lot of animals depend on this water. We don't want to disturb 'em any more than we have to."

They camped upstream in a mesquite bosque. Sam shot a large hare for their supper. He didn't think the noise made any difference now. He dressed the hare and cooked it over a small fire.

"That's the best meal I've had in a long time," Carolyn said when they were done eating.

Around them the light was fading fast. In the period just before final darkness an extraordinary quiet descended on the canyon. The air was ripe with the smell of wild mint. The campfire's reflection flickered across Carolyn's face as she looked at Sam archly. "Are we to have the same sleeping arrangements as last night, Mr. Slater?"

"Call me Sam," he said, and he moved beside her.

EVEN FROM A DISTANCE THE VILLAGE looked run-down.

"Let me handle things here," Sam told Carolyn as they viewed the village from a small height. "Give me some money. Not much—we don't want these people to know how much you got."

"Why?" she asked.

"*Bandidos.* They infest this country like bedbugs in a cheap hotel. They'll dig the gold out of your teeth. We've got to pretend we're down to our last few dollars."

Carolyn took twenty dollars in greenbacks

from her money belt and handed them to Sam. "Will that be enough?"

"That's plenty," Sam said. He crinkled the bills, then ground them into the dirt with his moccasin, to make them look well used. Then he put the bills in his pocket, and he and Carolyn went down into the village.

The village was not so much old as timeless, frozen in a moment of history. It centered on a square overgrown with weeds. In the center of the square was a copper fountain, green with neglect, that probably had not worked in fifty years. On the west side of the square was a church. Most of the square's other buildings were of tumbled-down adobe. Half-naked children chased bare-boned dogs, who in turn chased scrawny roosters and chickens. A cart, with one of its heavy wooden wheels missing, sat rotting in the sun. At one corner of the square lounged a sullen-looking fellow in a red serape, smoking a cigarito and pretending not to see the two gringos. Behind the village was a patch of indifferently cultivated ground where the older children kept busy by shooing goats out of the crops.

"This place gives a new meaning to the word 'sleepy,'" said Sam, looking around.

"'Comatose' is the word I'd use," said Carolyn. "I've seen more life in a corpse. Where are all the people?"

"Apaches have driven 'em away, like most of the villages in this part of Mexico."

"Do you really think we'll be able to buy animals here? Live ones, I mean?"

"We'll ask at the cantina."

The cantina's owner was as sleepy as the village. He was reluctant to talk at first, but after some persuasion he told Sam and Carolyn to inquire at the Casa Molina, at the far end of town.

"*Gracias,*" Sam told him. "What is this place called, anyway?"

"Santa Maria Navalmoral de la Mata," said the cantina's owner, puffing himself up proudly.

"Name's bigger than the town," remarked Sam. "*Gracias, amigo.*"

They found the Molina residence with no trouble. It was the biggest house in town, its plain walls fronting a courtyard that had seen better days. The courtyard gate was open, and a knock on the house door produced an elderly, part-Indian maid who instructed Sam and Carolyn to wait where they were.

The maid returned with a kindly-looking, silver-haired man, the picture of Castilian gentility. His short *charro* jacket and trousers had, like the house, seen better times, but if his penurious condition bothered him, he did not show it.

"*Bienvenido, amigos,*" the old man said, smiling and bowing gracefully. "I am Don Alejandro de Perez y Molina, at your service."

Sam returned the bow as best he could. "I'm Sam Slater. This is my . . . companion, Miss Manning."

"Señorita," Don Alejandro acknowledged, bowing again. "I am pleased to make your acquaintances. May I offer you refreshment? I have wine. Some fruit as well—apples, pears?"

"I don't know about the wine, but that fruit'd go down real good," Sam told him.

Don Alejandro issued instructions to the maid, then he led Sam and Carolyn across the courtyard to a bench and table shaded by an ancient pecan tree.

"Nice place," Sam observed.

Don Alejandro spread his hands apologetically. "I used to be a grand ranchero, you understand, but the Apache made it impossible to continue in that life. Now I do not do very much at all. I get few visitors here. You two are far from your homes, and you look as though you have seen—how do you say it up north?—the better days. What may I do for you?"

Sam said, "We're traveling to Arispe, and we had our horses stolen by Apaches. The fellow at the cantina said you might know where we could find fresh animals."

Don Alejandro pursed his lips. "Regrettably I have no horses. As happened to you, the Apache have stolen them all, save for my personal riding animals. I could, perhaps, provide you some mules." He paused, taking in Sam and Carolyn's tattered condition. "I do not wish to sound mercenary, but do you have money to pay for the mules?"

The maid brought a plate of fruit—apples,

pears, melon slices. Sam and Carolyn munched the sweet, thirst-quenching fruits greedily. "We have a little money," Sam said, wiping his mouth with the back of his hand. "As you can see, we're down on our luck."

"How much money?"

Sam wrinkled his forehead, seemingly embarrassed. "Fifteen dollars, American."

"And for that price do you also expect saddles and harness?"

"I'm afraid so. We have only a few dollars more, and we will need that to buy grain."

The old ranchero sighed. "Fifteen dollars. I would have hoped for more."

Carolyn felt sorry for the old man and she started to offer him more money, but Sam cut her off. "I'd like to be able to pay you more, but after we buy grain, we'll be busted flat."

Don Alejandro gave in. "Very well, I accept your price. I do not like to see two people such as yourselves in these unfortunate circumstances."

While the mules were sent for Sam pulled out the dirty, crinkled greenbacks. He smoothed and counted them, then handed fifteen to Don Alejandro. Folding the money, Don Alejandro studied Carolyn carefully. "Miss Manning's feet, they are in bad condition."

Sam agreed. "I'm hoping to find her a pair of *guaraches* while we're here."

"I have something better, I believe." The old man disappeared into the house and returned with a worn but well-cared-for pair of riding boots. He handed them to Carolyn. "Try these on. They belonged to my daughter."

Carolyn said, "Oh, no, I couldn't. . . ."

Don Alejandro held up a hand. "It is all right. She is dead. She died in the childbirth some years ago."

"Oh," said Carolyn. "I'm sorry."

"*Por favor*, take them. I would prefer that they do someone good."

Carolyn tried on the boots. They were supple and well broken in, and with a childlike cry of joy she discovered that they fit.

Don Alejandro smiled at her. "Would you care to try on some of her clothing as well?" He motioned to the elderly maid. "Estella, take Miss Manning to my daughter's room. Let her pick out some of Maria's traveling clothes."

"Sí, patrón," said the maid, and she led Carolyn into the house.

While they were gone, Sam said to Don Alejandro, "Has a group of *americanos* been through here lately? Four men?"

The old man nodded. "*Sí.* They have been in Santa Maria. These men, they are dangerous. They have a woman with them. They treat her very badly, I think. You know them?"

"I'm fixin' to."

"My advice to you would be to stay away from these men, señor."

Sam made no response to that. He said, "Is the road to Arispe safe from *bandidos*?"

"There are two roads to Arispe. The main one

runs directly south from here across the tableland. The other winds through the eastern hills. I would advise you to take the longer road through the hills. The flatland is, as you say, a hunting ground for *bandidos* who ambush unwary travelers."

"We'll do that," Sam said.

The old man went on. "If I may also suggest —I hope you do not resent these endless suggestions—you might even start on the southern road, then switch to the hills once you are no longer in sight of the town. The *bandidos* have friends in Santa Maria. It may be that they will follow you from here."

"Good idea. Is there any water before the Rancho Alvarado?"

"Ah, so you know the Rancho Alvarado?"

Sam was noncommittal. "I know of it. It's about thirty-five miles south of here, isn't it?"

"About that, yes, and regrettably there is no water before you reach there."

Two saddled mules were brought forth by the don's servants. At the same time Carolyn came back, combed and cleaned up somewhat, and wearing a fresh set of riding clothes. The elderly maid followed a few steps behind her. The maid caught Don Alejandro's eye and nodded to him.

"Muy perfecto," Don Alejandro said, smiling at Carolyn. "Now you are truly ready for your journey." He gave Sam a hand. "*Vaya con Dios, mis amigos.*"

"Gracias," said Sam. "Thanks for your help."

"Thank you for everything," said Carolyn. "Good-bye."

Before leaving the village, Sam and Carolyn purchased grain for the mules. In the square the sullen-looking fellow in the red serape had not moved. Once again he pretended not to be watching the two gringos, but Sam knew that he was. Strangers like Sam and Carolyn could not go through a small town like this without attracting attention. Just the manner in which the man was going out of his way to show indifference was suspicious.

Taking Don Alejandro's advice, Sam and Carolyn started south across the tableland, and when they were several miles from the village, they turned east, hiding their trail, and headed into the mountains.

They found the mountain road easily enough. It was more of a track than a road as it wound among the rugged hills. At one point it ran along a steep cliffside, with an almost sheer drop to the left. Sam and Carolyn rode their mules single file along the narrow path, with Sam in the lead. The afternoon was hot; the canyon was silent. Carolyn hugged the cliff wall, looking nervous.

"What's the matter?" Sam asked her.

"I'm afraid of heights," she confessed.

Just then they rounded a bend of the canyon wall, to find a group of armed men blocking the trail in front of them. The men were heavily armed, mounted on shaggy ponies. At their head was the man in the red serape from the village.

"Bandidos," Sam swore.

He urged his mule around on the narrow path. "Come on," he told Carolyn.

The two of them retreated along the canyon wall, with the bandits following slowly. As Sam and Carolyn rounded another bend they found their path blocked in that direction as well.

The bandits were to their front and rear. On one side of them the drop was almost perpendicular, on the other side was a towering rock wall. Sam spied a V-shaped niche along the rock wall, with a fall of boulders. "Over there," he told Carolyn.

They kicked their mules into the niche and dismounted, taking cover among the boulders. As the first gunshots sounded from the *bandidos* Sam took his rifle and tossed his pistol to Carolyn. He cocked his rifle, aimed, and fired. One of the *bandidos* fell from his horse to the ground. The others took cover along the rock wall and opened fire. Sam and Carolyn ducked their heads as bullets whined off the rock around them.

"Aren't you going to do something?" Carolyn asked Sam.

"Do what?" said Sam. "This ain't one of Ned Buntline's Wild West spectaculars. There's at least twenty of them. We can't fight our way out, and there's nowhere to run if we could. They got us dead."

"Hey, gringo," cried a voice. "How you two doin' in there?"

"I've done better," Sam called back.

"Tha's a funny answer, gringo. We got you in the trap good, I think."

Sam peeked over the rocks. The speaker was their old friend in the red serape. The bandit went on. "I tell you what, gringo. Give us your money, and we let you and the woman go."

"Do we look like people that have money?" Sam called back. "You picked the wrong people to rob, amigo."

"I don' think tha's true," said the *bandido*. "I think you got more money than you pretend to. Now, are you goin' to give it to us, or do we got to take it?"

Next to Sam Carolyn said, "What are we going to do?"

Sam swore to himself. "If it was just the money, I'd let you have it," he told the bandit, "but I think you want the woman, too; and if you do, you'll have to fight."

"I tol' you, we let the woman go."

"How do I know you're telling the truth?"

"You have my word upon it," said another voice, and Don Alejandro Molina rode around the corner of the canyon, coming to a stop beside the first bandit.

"Don Alejandro," gasped Carolyn.

The old man spread his hands with that apologetic air. "Yes."

Carolyn stood up. "You're one of the *bandidos*?"

"In these lean times one does what one can to survive."

"You set us up," she said. "While we were going from one trail to the other, your men had time to get in front of us and ambush us."

"This is true. Regrettably, from your standpoint."

"But you, of all people, should know that we don't have any money."

Don Alejandro smiled. "While you were changing your clothes, Miss Manning, my maid watched you. She reported that you are in possession of a very well-stocked money belt, which I now must ask you to turn over to me."

"And if we don't?" Sam said.

"The price, I am afraid, will be your lives. So you see, you have no choice."

Sam sighed and motioned to Carolyn. "Go ahead."

Carolyn removed the money belt from her skirt. Dismounting, Don Alejandro came forward, and she handed the belt to him. "I must ask for your firearms as well," the old man said.

"Our guns?" Sam protested. "But you'll be leaving us defenseless."

"I am sorry, but I cannot have you coming back to Santa Maria to shoot me. Besides, your guns are valuable. They are better than anything my men have. Once again I am afraid you have no choice."

Sam swore. Then he tossed his Winchester and shell belt to Don Alejandro, who caught them deftly. Carolyn handed the old man the pistol.

"You may keep your knife," Don Alejandro told Sam.

"Hooray," cracked Sam. "I suppose you want the mules, too?"

"Yes, why not? Perhaps I can sell them again, to the next gringos who come through here."

Don Alejandro's men laughed at this remark. Sam and Carolyn did not find it as funny.

The old man went on. "Miss Manning, you may keep my daughter's clothing. I mean no injury to you. This is—how do you say it?—business. I wish you good luck on the remainder of your journey."

"You have a strange way of showing it," Carolyn told him.

Don Alejandro laid the money belt across his saddle. He handed the rifle and pistol to his accomplice from the village. Another *bandido* took the mules, leaving the canteens. To Sam and Carolyn Don Alejandro said, "And now, my friends, we will bid you *adios*."

He remounted his horse. Some of the bandits began shooting off their weapons in celebration, but a look from the old don silenced them. The bandits rode back down the cliffside trail, toward Santa Maria, leaving Sam and Carolyn by the boulders.

When the *bandidos* were gone, Sam took off his hat and slapped dust from his trousers. "No guns, no money, no mules. Damn." He looked over at Carolyn, who was staring straight ahead, lips trembling. "You ain't goin' to start crying on me now, are you? 'Cause if there's anything I hate, it's weepy—"

"Oh, for heaven's sake, I'm not going to cry. I'm trying to think, if you'd stop your infernal chatter."

"Well, while you're thinking so hard, suppose you tell me what we're going to do next?"

Carolyn looked at him forthrightly. "I don't know about you, but I intend to continue after Gus Grissom."

"How are we supposed to take Grissom and his gang without guns?"

"We'll find a way."

"What about that reward you promised? How will you pay me now that your money's gone?"

Carolyn looked thoughtful. "Grissom has the money he stole from the bank . . . ?"

"I couldn't take that money. You know that."

"Yes, of course. It was just a thought."

"Like you said, I don't have many virtues," Sam reminded, "but honesty's one of them."

"What about those Texas rewards on Grissom and his men?"

"Getting those fellows back from Mexico to Texas—especially if they're dead—could be a problem. I don't know if it's worth what the Texans are paying for them."

They stood there for a minute, then Sam said, "You're bound to do this, aren't you?"

"Yes, Sam. I am."

Sam thought about Carolyn's dead father and brother. He thought about the dead rancher's kidnapped wife, whom he had never seen. She had been on his mind since he had first learned about her. Don Alejandro had said she was still alive and was being treated badly. What did he owe her—what did he owe Carolyn?

He let out his breath. "Then I guess I'm coming with you."

Carolyn smiled. "You once said that you don't work for free."

"There's a first time for everything," Sam told her. "Come on, let's get moving, before I smarten up and change my mind."

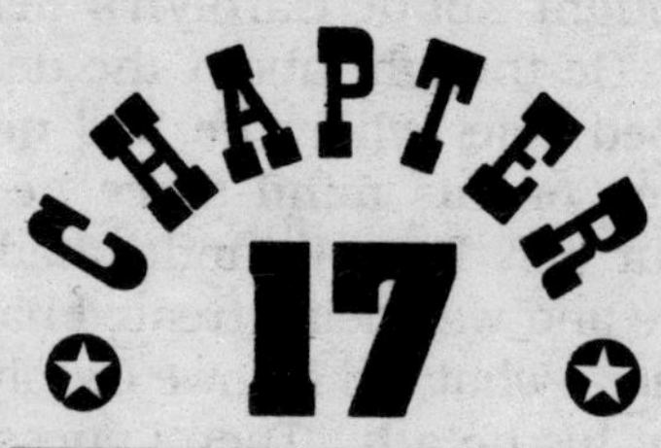

SAM AND CAROLYN HIKED DEEPER INTO THE rugged Mexican mountains. "How are your feet?" Sam asked.

"They still hurt," Carolyn admitted, though she did her best not to show the pain. "But these new boots help."

Carolyn had liked Don Alejandro, and she was bitter about the way he had tricked them. "That old . . ." She stopped for want of a word that she could say in public. After pausing to collect herself, she went on: "He didn't mind picking on us, but I notice that he and his big, brave *bandidos* left the Grissom gang alone. I guess Grissom had too many men for them, too many guns."

"That should tell you something," Sam commented. "We're proposing to take on Grissom with two people and no guns."

Her green eyes glared at him. "You can always back out."

"I ain't big on backing out," Sam replied.

They continued on.

They camped early, then walked for much of the night to avoid the heat and conserve water, which was again running low. The next morning the trail came down from the mountains and met the rutted track that served as a road over the tableland.

Sam stopped and examined the road closely.

"What is it?" asked Carolyn.

"Tracks, of four horses. One of 'em's being ridden double."

Sam walked along, following the tracks, which Carolyn couldn't distinguish from the hundreds of other tracks in the path. At one point the tracks strayed into some grass by the side of the road. Sam cut one of the bent blades of grass and tasted the juice with the tip of his tongue. At another point he cut into a pile of manure and examined the insides.

"It's Grissom's men," he said at last. "We're no more than a day behind them."

"What happened to their other horse?"

Sam shrugged. "Could have been anything. Went lame and had to be put down, most likely. It happened since they left Santa Maria, or they would have gotten a remount there."

"At least it's slowed them down. That's good for us, isn't it?"

"It helps, but not that much. The Rancho Alvarado's a big outfit. They'll be able to get a fresh horse there."

Carolyn looked at him quizzically. "You sound like you've been to this Rancho Alvarado before."

"I have."

He decided that he owed her an explanation, and as they started walking again he said, "I was sixteen, living with the Apaches. It was my first raid as a warrior."

The events of that long-ago night came back as if they were happening all over again. "I was scared as . . . well, let's just say I was plenty scared. At that age I should only have been an apprentice warrior, but I'd proved my worth early when my band was attacked by Mexicans. Some of the older warriors resented me, because of my age and the fact I was white. They were looking for me to fail, and that didn't make me feel any easier.

"We were after horses. My job was to sneak close and open the corral. The corral was adobe, with a barred wooden gate. There was a lock on the gate and I couldn't open it, so I took a rope and went over the top. I passed one end of the rope to my partner on the other side. He's dead now, and Apache custom forbids me to speak his name. The two of us used the rope like a saw, and we cut through the mortar between the adobe blocks. We tore a hole in the wall, then the rest of our men came through. One of the Mexican guards spotted us and came running up, shooting off an old blunderbuss. He was a kid, about the same age as me. I killed him with my bow."

Sam paused, then went on. "We ran off the horse herd, and the Mexicans chased us, but their flintlocks and blunderbusses were no good against our bows, not in this country. We ambushed 'em, killed a bunch, and the rest retreated. My first raid . . ."

His voice trailed off, and he added, "I still think of that guard sometimes."

"Why did you kill him?" Carolyn asked.

"I was an Apache, living Apache ways. My people had raided this rancho for generations, sometimes for horses, sometimes to kill the men and carry off women and children. They were the enemy, the *inda.*"

"They had to defend their property," Carolyn pointed out.

Sam smiled thinly. "My Apache father would have told you that we were defending *our* property."

"What property?"

"This land," Sam said.

At the noon break they finished their water. "Here we go again," said Sam, draining his canteen.

Carolyn said, "Just for once I wish we'd find a trail that ran alongside a river."

"There's a spring at the rancho. We'll get

water there. If we're lucky, maybe they'll lend us some horses, too." Sam paused. "I'm going to feel funny begging those people for their hospitality when the last time I was there I was stealing their stock."

"It's not like they're going to remember you," Carolyn pointed out.

"I'll remember," Sam said. "That's what's important."

The Rancho Alvarado lay in a pass between two short mountain ranges. The road to Arispe wound through the pass as well. It was the hottest part of the afternoon when Sam and Carolyn entered the twisting pass. Carolyn kept her eyes focused in front of her, eager for the first sight of water. She noticed Sam's expression as he looked around the rocky sides of the pass.

"Why the long face?" she asked him.

"I don't know," he replied. "It's been a good many years since I was through here. It hasn't changed much. Not far from here's where we ambushed the Mexicans. Seems like everywhere I go, people die."

Further on, the pass twisted around a long spur of the mountains. Sam said, "The rancho is just around that spur."

"Finally," said Carolyn, picking up the pace. "I'm dying for water, a hot meal, maybe even a bath and a night's sleep under a real roof."

"Wait," Sam told her.

She looked at him.

"You stay here. I'm going to scout the area."

"Why? It seems safe enough."

He made a cautionary gesture. "Old habits die hard."

Sam climbed the mountain spur, crossing it nimbly, feeling strangely at home as he moved from rock to rock. He might have been wearing a breechclout and headband once more, and been carrying a bow in his hand instead of a Winchester repeater.

As he neared the ridge he slowed. He sank to the ground and crept on his stomach, waiting for the rancho to come into view below him.

The rancho had been built near a large underground spring. The spring's year-round water supply and its lush gramma grasses provided grazing for horses and cattle. The ranch buildings themselves, Sam remembered, were set back about four hundred yards from the spring, on a rise of ground leading into the mountains. In his mind's eye he was prepared for the vigorous, thriving community of his past, full of people and animals. What he saw made him take in his breath.

The old rancho had been abandoned. The fortresslike adobe buildings were without their roofs and parts of their walls. The corrals had fallen down. The neat gardens and outbuildings had disappeared entirely. The area was overrun with weeds and mesquite.

Once the ranch had been a prosperous, thriving entity. Now all that was gone. Sam's people, the Apache, were responsible. They had killed the rancho's inhabitants or driven them off.

His people had won.

In a way Sam supposed that he should feel a sense of triumph, but he didn't. He felt only sadness.

Then he came back to his senses, and on second inspection he realized that the rancho was abandoned but not deserted. Four horses rested peacefully in the ruins of one of the corrals. In what remained of the old ranch building, five people were camped—four men and a woman. Even at this distance Sam could tell that two of the men were quarreling—presumably over the woman. The other two were doing their best to stay out of the argument.

The woman seemed to have been terribly abused. The sight sickened Sam, but there was nothing he could do about it. As he watched, one of the men dragged her off into a corner of the tumbledown building. Sam turned away, unable to look anymore.

He made his way back to where Carolyn waited. "I think we've found Gus Grissom and his gang."

He led Carolyn back over the spur, and the two of them looked down on the deserted ranch and the men camped there. Carolyn's mouth was a hard line. Her chest rose and fell; her breath came in short bursts.

"That's them," she said.

"You're sure?" Sam asked.

"I was there the day they killed my father and brother. I'm sure."

Sam motioned her away from the crest. "Now what?" she said.

Sam was grim, businesslike. "After dark I'm going to sneak in there and kill them."

Their eyes met. "That's—that's rather extreme, isn't it?" Carolyn said.

"I'm in a rather extreme kind of profession," Sam replied.

When they returned to the far side of the spur, Sam began carefully rubbing more dirt onto his already filthy undershirt and trousers. He rubbed dirt on his face and in his hair as well, until he was the color of earth from head to foot. Then he tied his bandanna around his longish hair to keep it out of his eyes. "Stay here," he told Carolyn.

"What are you going to do?" she asked.

"I'm going down to the ranch."

WHEN VIRGE WAS FINISHED WITH BETH McNally, he swaggered back to the little group of men in the ruined adobe ranch house. It was late afternoon, and the men were sitting around a fire, drinking coffee and eating tortillas and beans that they had purchased at that greaser village. Virge buckled his gun belt back on, making a big point of seating the holster properly on his hip.

"Man, I never had me a woman like that," he bragged.

Cherokee Bill was not impressed. "You mean, one who's half-dead?"

"I mean one who's that good, Chief."

Bill's features grew even meaner than usual. "Don't call me 'Chief,' cowboy. My name's Bill."

Virge slapped his pistol butt arrogantly. "I reckon this here gives me the right to call you just about anything I choose."

Bill eased the barrels of his sawed-off shotgun across his lap and into firing position. "You think so? This scattergun would blow your skinny ass in half."

"Enough, you two!" said Paco, standing. The ponytailed ex-vaquero was angry. "*Madre de Dios*, I knew we should not have brought the woman with us. Gus, I told you that."

"Too late to fix things now," Gus said.

Gus got up and strolled over to where the McNally woman huddled against the crumbled wall. Her clothes were all askew from her latest pawing by Virge. Gus pulled down her skirt and straightened her blouse as best he could. He gave her a tin plate with some folded tortillas and beans and a cup of coffee.

"Here," he said.

She took the plate without looking at him. She no longer flinched from his gaze or touch. She acted like he wasn't there. She acted like *she* wasn't there. It was like she was dead inside. Kind of a waste, Gus thought as he shook his head and started back.

After the woman had been recaptured, Gus had beaten her, not enough to do real damage—he didn't want to lower her market value—but enough to make sure she didn't run away again. Afterward they'd had to tie her on her horse so she didn't fall off.

The woman and the rest of Gus's party had attracted a lot of attention in the greaser village—Gus had no idea what its name was, and cared less—but the greasers had been able to do no more than look. Gus and his men had them outgunned. Gus had wanted to speed up on the tableland, but the woman had held them back. Then Virge's horse had been bitten by a rattler while grazing. The horse had run off, stepped in a hole and cracked its foreleg, then had to be shot. Virge had taken turns riding double with the others till they got to this old rancho.

Virge had been in a sulk ever since his run-in with Gus. They would be staying at the rancho for the day to rest the horses, so Gus had relented and let Virge have the woman. Now he was wishing that he hadn't.

Gus returned to the rest of the gang. Virge had grown testy and sullen again.

Gus swore to himself. "Go on," he told Virge. "Say it. Let's have this out once and for all."

Virge looked at Gus from under half-lowered eyelids. "I still don't want you to sell her."

"What is it with you and this woman?" said Gus. "Are you in love with her?"

Virge hemmed and hawed. "Well, I don't know much about love, but I kind of like her. I feel like she should be mine, you know?"

"No. I don't know."

"I can't rightly explain it. I just don't want to let her go."

"Jesus, Virge, you're either crazy or you're stupider than you look. What makes you think she's going to fall for you? After the way we treated her?"

Virge got his back up. "I reckon she could. I don't want to sell her, is all."

"And I do," Gus said.

Virge got to his feet. "You ain't gettin' the drop on me unawares this time, Gus."

"I don't need to, you pea-brained—"

Cherokee Bill stepped between them. "I've had you two. Damn people arguin' over a damn bitch. Stupidest damn thing I ever seen. You settle this right now, one way or the other."

Gus kept his eyes on Virge, and he kept his hand near his pistol. "That's what we was fixin' to do."

The big breed went on. "I got a way to do it, won't get one of you fools kilt. Not that I care, but we're supposed to be partners."

"What is it?" Gus said.

Bill pulled out a deck of cards. "Cut for her. The winner keeps her, and that's an end to it."

Gus didn't like it. He was supposed to be the leader here. But it was better than swapping shots with Virge. The ex-cowboy was good with a gun, real good, and Gus wasn't sure he would win against him. "It's all right with me," he said at last. "Virge?"

"I'm game," said the skinny blond.

Gus and Virge sat by the fire again. Bill squatted beside them and laid down the greasy, dog-eared cards.

Gus started to pick up the deck, but Virge said, "Wait. Bill, you shuffle."

Gus looked at him. "What's wrong? Don't trust me?"

"Hell, no, I don't trust you. You lived with that saloon whore for a year and a half. You prob'ly know every card trick there is."

Gus smiled and nodded to Bill, who picked up the cards and shuffled them laboriously with his thick fingers. Leaning against the adobe wall, Beth McNally watched without interest, even though she knew they were gambling for her. She didn't see what difference the outcome made. Either way this was a nightmare from which there was no escape.

When Bill was done shuffling, he handed the deck to Paco. "Cut?"

Paco knelt and cut the deck. Bill evened the edges, then placed the cards between Gus and Virge.

"You first," Gus told Virge.

Virge hesitated. He snatched up part of the deck and showed the card.

"Queen Victoria, queen of hearts," he crowed, laughing. He replaced the cards, squaring the edges. "Come on, Gus. Let's see you beat that."

Gus was tight-lipped, his jaw muscles working. He put a hand on the deck, settled it, then lifted.

It was the king of clubs.

A grin spread across Gus's darkly handsome face. "That's it. Fair and square."

Cherokee Bill looked at both of them. "No more arguin' now. Agreed?"

Virge was breathing hard, but he said, "Agreed."

Gus stood, gave the cards back to Bill, and turned away. As he did so Virge drew his pistol. He stepped forward and hit Gus across the back of the head with the pistol barrel.

"Ow!" Gus said, grabbing at his head. Virge hit him again, and Gus sank to his knees. He remained there, holding his head, with blood trickling through his fingers and matting his dark hair.

Virge pointed his pistol at Paco and Cherokee Bill. "This here is 'tween me and Gus. You two keep out, and we won't have no trouble."

The two men moved back. They put their hands up. "Easy, Virge," said Bill.

Virge indicated Gus. "Tie him up, Paco. Tie his hands behind him."

Paco said, "Virge, you are—"

"Do it!"

"All right, all right. I do it." Paco fetched a length of rope. Virge was crazy; Paco had known it all along. He had never wanted the Texan in the gang, but Gus had been so impressed by Virge's ability with a gun that he'd been willing to overlook all his other drawbacks. Well, now those drawbacks were coming home to roost, and Gus was their victim.

With his boot Virge pushed the moaning Gus flat on the ground. Paco bent and tied Gus's hands behind him. "I'm sorry, Señor Gus. You understand, it is nothing personal."

"Take his gun, too," Virge ordered, and Paco complied.

Gus rolled over and lifted his head, grimacing with pain as he looked at Virge. "What's your plan, Virge, besides to screw that woman every fifteen minutes?"

"I ain't got that part figured out yet, but she's mine."

Gus went on. "You know I'm not going to let you get away with this."

"Shut up, Gus, or by God I'll shoot you."

He meant it. Gus was quiet. Virge walked over to the McNally woman. "Come here, darlin'. Sit next to your uncle Virge."

Beth did as she was told. The fog that had shrouded her brain lifted for a second, and she felt almost relieved, because it occurred to her that she had just received a death sentence, and because of that an end to her ordeal was in sight. Gus would have sold her to the Mexicans and an eternity of hell, but Virge would kill her when he grew tired of her—as he was bound to do when his childish romantic fantasies wore off.

As Beth sat beside him Virge put an arm around her shoulder and toyed with one of her breasts. He looked at Gus, rubbing it in.

Cherokee Bill stood, patting his gut. "These

beans is gettin' to me. I gotta go. Ain't gonna interfere none with your love life, is it, Romeo?"

"Go on," said Virge. "Git."

In deference to the woman's presence, the gang was using as a latrine a stand of oaks below the rise and off to the right of the ruined ranch buildings. To get there Bill had to cross a field of foot-high grass clumped with cudweed.

Bill had decided to leave this circus when they got to Arispe. He wished he'd never joined the outfit—though he had to admit, he'd made more money with Gus than on all the jobs he'd done by himself put together. He was a loner by nature, though, and working with a gang went against his grain.

Bill had acquired quite a reputation up in the Indian Territory—for horse-and-cattle stealing, robbery, and murder. When the Nations had grown too hot for him, he had hightailed it to Texas, where he'd met Gus Grissom in a Fort Griffin saloon. Gus had told him his plans for robbing banks, and Bill had signed on.

Gus had shown Bill where the real money lay and how to get it, and Bill would always be grateful for that, but after this he was going back to working alone. He certainly wasn't going to waste time lying around some greaser town with the rest of them, arguing over women. He would go back up to the Nations. He would be at home there, among his own people, and he would pick up where he had . . .

He stopped. He was in the middle of the

grassy field. A white man wouldn't have noticed anything, but the Indian in Bill told him something was wrong. Bill's mother had been a Cherokee; he had been told that his father was an army deserter—though he never knew whether from the Union or Confederate side.

Now he looked around, searching the springs, the pass, the mountains. All seemed normal, but something just didn't feel right. He looked back at the ranch buildings, then at the field of high grass surrounding him, and finally right at his feet. . . .

He barely saw the arm that reached up from the tall grass, grabbed him, and dragged him down. An iron grip clamped his mouth shut to keep him from crying out. As he began thrashing he felt a sharp pain as a blade was thrust under his breastbone and into his heart. He tried to scream, but his face was ground into the dirt by a strength even greater than his own, which surprised him, and he wondered who it could be, even as he knew that he couldn't breathe. He couldn't breathe at all. . . .

Paco left the campfire. He was thinking of his woman, Elena, in Arispe. The more time Gus and Virge played with this gringo woman, the longer it was taking him to get back to Elena. After this he would ride no more with the gringos. He would take his share of the money, and he would buy a fine house. He and Elena would open up a grand *fonda,* what the gringos called a restaurant. He would pour the drinks and she would serve the food, and the two of them would spend the rest of their days in peace and contentment. And if, from time to time, he enjoyed other women on the side, Elena would not mind, for that was the way of a man.

Paco leaned idly against the ruined wall, facing the stand of oaks. He wondered where Bill could have gone. There was no sign of him, and he shouldn't be out of sight already. There was only a slight ripple in the long grass, which Paco thought odd because there was no wind. But the ripple died, and Paco paid it no more attention.

When he was satisfied that the big man was dead, Sam twisted his knife free of the man's chest. Still lying concealed in the grass, he wiped the blade with dirt and sheathed it. Sam had stuck grass in his hair and headband, on his undershirt and trousers, until he blended in perfectly with the field. He hadn't wanted to kill anyone—not yet. He had been spying on the bandits' camp, getting in position to move when it got dark. Ordinarily he might have remained up on the mountain spur, then come down after dark, but the kidnapped woman's presence changed things. Sam had decided to try to get her out first, before all hell broke loose.

Sam's presence would never have been detected if this big man had not come along. The big man had practically walked on top of him. Even then, Sam had managed to avoid being seen until the man looked down. Sam cursed his luck—ninety-nine out of a hundred men would have kept on going. Even worse, the man had not been carrying a gun that Sam could use. The bandits were going to know there was something wrong now. Sam was not going to be able to wait until dark to make his move.

On the rise Gus sat with his back to the ruined wall, teeth clenched against the pain pulsing through his head. He was lucky his skull hadn't been broken by the force of Virge's blows. Nearby, Virge giggled at Beth McNally, who looked anywhere but at him. Virge ran his fingertips up and down her arm, as though she were some sort of exotic new pet. "I'd rather have you than the money," he told her. "I swear I would."

"Virge, you're an idiot," Gus said. "You're making a fool of yourself over a piece of ass. What do you intend on doing with me?"

Virge glared at him. "I ain't figured that part out yet, neither."

"I do not see Bill," Paco said, interrupting them.

"Huh?" said Virge.

Paco was still looking toward the oaks. "Bill. He has been gone a long time. I do not see him."

"He's over by them trees takin' a"—Virge

remembered that a lady was present, and he changed his words—"relieving hisself."

"No, he is *not*," Paco replied, and there was a worried note in his voice that got Virge's attention. "He should not be gone this long. Something has happened. He has vanished."

Virge stood and walked over beside the ex-vaquero. The westering sun had turned the long grass golden; the shadows in the pass were lengthening. The old rancho was quiet.

Paco swallowed. "I do not like this."

Behind them Gus grinned and said, "Better untie me, Virge. Looks like you got yourself some trouble."

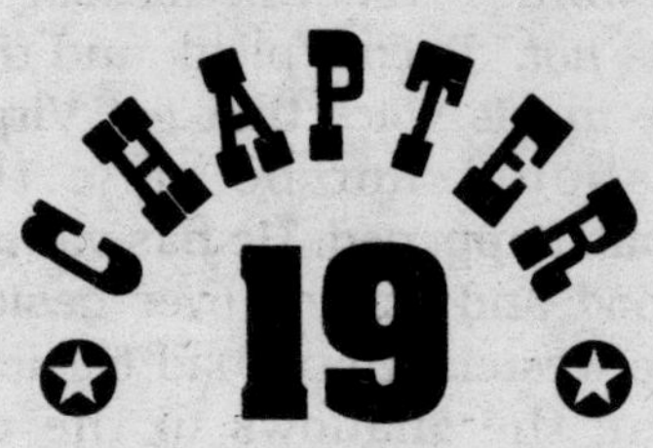

VIRGE HESITATED, THEN HE DREW HIS KNIFE and cut the rope that bound Gus's hands. Nearby, Beth McNally looked up, showing interest in what was going on for the first time since her recapture.

Gus stood, rubbing his wrists and shaking his head as though to rid it of the pain from being hit with Virge's gun barrel—though he quickly learned what a mistake that was.

Virge watched him and backed away, warily.

"Don't worry," Gus told him. "I ain't going to shoot you. Yet."

Gus walked to the crumbling adobe wall and

stood beside Paco, his sharp eyes surveying the quiet scene around the spring and the old rancho. He looked from one end of the pass—or valley, really, it was so wide—to the other. Aside from the horses in the old corral, nothing moved.

"Bill!" Gus's shout hung in the late-afternoon air and echoed faintly off the mountains.

He tried again. "Bill! Where the hell are you?"

There was no answer.

"What do you think happened to him?" asked Virge, coming up beside them.

"I don't know," Gus replied.

"Was it Apaches?"

Looking toward the pass, Paco said, "I do not think so. I cannot tell you why, but I do not think it."

Virge went on. "Me, I say it's that bunch that did for the posse."

Gus wasn't sure. "I figured we were rid of them once we hit that greaser village."

"Don't know who else it could be, do you?"

Gus seemed to feel a shadow cross his soul, but he shivered and the feeling went away. "No," he said, and he called out again. "Bill! Damn you, answer!"

The quiet of the pass was disturbed only by the receding echoes. Finally Gus turned to Virge. "You got ideas about bossing this outfit, Virge. What's our play?"

Virge was forced to own up to his inadequacies. Thinking and planning were not his strong suits. "Hell, Gus, I don't know."

"I didn't figure you would."

Virge dug a hole in the dirt with the high heel of his cowboy boot. "You're still boss, Gus. I just wanted the girl, is all."

"Get my rifle and pistol."

"Sure, Gus. Sure." Virge seemed relieved to have things back to normal. He seemed relieved to have somebody else taking responsibility for what was going to happen. He returned and handed Gus his guns. "I'm sorry I hit you. It's just that I—"

"Save it for later," Gus told him. "We got more important things to worry about just now." He stuck the pistol in its holster and levered a shell into the chamber of his Winchester.

Paco was also glad to see Gus back in charge. "What shall we do, Señor Gus?"

"The first thing we're going to do is find out what happened to Bill."

"One of us better stay and watch the woman," Virge suggested.

"No," said Gus, "I don't want us splitting up. Divide and conquer, that's the first rule in war. We'll tie her so she can't get away again. Go on, Virge, you handle that."

Virge went over and bound Beth's hands and feet with short lengths of rope. "Nothing to say to me?" he asked her as he worked. "No lover's farewell?"

Beth glared at him with contempt.

"That's all right." Virge chuckled. "It ain't no matter. You'll talk to me someday. You'll like me, you'll see."

He finished with the ropes and stood up. "Don't go away now," he told Beth, winking. Then he joined the others.

The three bandits started off the rise. Gus and Virge carried rifles; Paco had taken Cherokee Bill's sawed-off shotgun. "Spread out," Gus told them.

They headed for the stand of oaks, moving through the grass and cudweed, feeling it whip round their ankles. Their nervous eyes searched the rangeland and mountains beyond the oaks.

"I don't see him," Virge said.

Paco crossed himself. "It is like he has vanished from the face of the earth."

Gus was more of a realist. "Yeah, well, we all know that ain't possible. People just don't—"

"Hey! What the . . . !" Virge stumbled over something in the thick grass. He looked down. "Christ. It's Bill."

The others joined him. The big breed lay facedown, unmoving. There was blood in the dirt beneath him. Gus knelt and turned him over, revealing a blood-soaked wound under his breastbone. Bill's dead eyes stared wide in fear and surprise.

"Jesus," Virge said.

Gus let the body fall back, and he stood. The three bandits looked around, fingering the triggers of their weapons. The mountains, the rancho, the land around them—all were quiet.

Paco found faint tracks in the long grass, where the killer had backed away. "Look here," he said.

Gus examined the tracks. "Virge was right," he said. "It *was* Apaches done this. Had to be."

Virge looked around wildly, as if he expected the Apaches to materialize out of the ground beside him. "Where are they? Where'd they go?"

"All right, all right, keep your head," Gus told him. "Panicking's what they want us to do. Come on, we better get back to the camp."

Sam backed out of the grassy field. The remaining bandits would soon come looking for their companion, and Sam had nothing but his knife to fight them with. If only that big fellow had been carrying a gun, it would have helped to even the odds a bit.

Sam moved swiftly and silently, and when the grass thinned, he turned and headed back up the spur of the mountain. The bandits would guess that Apaches killed their friend. Sam figured the first thing they would do would be to try to get away. Sam had wanted to free that woman prisoner, but he decided to forget her for a moment and concentrate on the bandits' horses. If he could run off the horses, he could keep the bandits here, or at least keep them from getting a big lead on himself and Carolyn.

The horses wouldn't go far, because the spring was the only source of water for miles around. For the same reason the animals would eventually return to the spring on their own. Sam intended to tie them somewhere out of the way and make the bandits come for them. That would give him a chance either to split the bandits up or to pick them off one by one.

He crossed the crest of the spur and came in behind the rancho, moving silently down the mountainside, using the cover of brush and rocks. Below, he saw the three surviving bandits look toward the field where the dead breed lay. He heard them call the man's name. "Bill." Well, at least now he had a name to put with the dead man's murderous face.

The bandits took their guns and left the ruined ranch house. More bad luck for Sam—they weren't leaving a guard on either the horses or the woman. If they had, Sam could have overpowered him and obtained a gun, besides reducing the enemy's number by one more.

Sam made his way toward the old adobe corral and the four horses inside. He circled the corral to come in downwind of the horses. It was the same way he had approached the corral those many years before, and he felt ghosts all around him—ghosts of the once-great rancho, ghosts of the Apaches with whom he had come here that night—Loco, his adopted father, killed by the American army; Born of Water, his partner at the corral wall, dead of the white man's smallpox. Shimmering before his eyes, he seemed to see once more the young guard he had killed. That boy would have been about Sam's own age today, had he lived. But he hadn't lived, and it was because of Sam that he hadn't.

Sam shook off the feeling. He had to keep his mind on what he was doing. The past was past. That boy would have killed Sam if he'd been able to.

The corral's massive wooden gate, whose lock had frustrated Sam on that long-ago night, had disappeared. The bandits had strung a picket rope across the entrance to keep their horses inside. There would have been no need to climb over the walls this time, either. There was not enough wall left.

With his knife Sam cut the picket rope. From the field behind him he heard a loud exclamation. The bandits must have found their dead friend.

Sam slipped off his undershirt and entered the corral, circling the walls downwind. The horses snorted and pawed the ground at his presence, and he spoke to them soothingly in Apache. He drew closer, still talking low. He came to the first horse, a dull chestnut, and stroked its muzzle. *"Enjuh, enjuh,"* he murmured. Then he grabbed the horse's mane and vaulted onto its back.

"Yah!" he yelled, waving his shirt at the other horses. "Yah! Yah!"

The horses whinnied, one of them reared. Sam swung around on the chestnut, heading the horses for the open corral gate. "Yah! Yah!"

"Look!" came a cry from below. "The horses!"

Sam rode out the gate behind the horses, waving the shirt and yelling at them, starting them up the pass toward Arispe. From behind him there were rifle shots. The loud reports spooked the horses and made them run faster.

More shots rang out. Sam put his head down, riding hard. He saw figures running toward him, cursing and firing rifles.

Suddenly the chestnut reared, screaming, and crashed to the ground. Sam just managed to scramble free of the falling animal, twisting his ankle as he did so. A cloud of dust blew around him, giving him momentary cover. The chestnut was done for; Sam couldn't get it back to its feet. The other horses were too far gone to catch. The bandits were coming closer, and Sam heard one of them cry, "It's an Injun!"

"No, it ain't," yelled another. "Lookit them pants. That's a white man!"

Puffs of dirt kicked up all around Sam from the rifle bullets flying his way. He hobbled back toward the mountain, with the bandits in pursuit.

Sam's ankle warmed up as he ran. His strides grew longer. He reached the mountain and started up, taking advantage of every dip and fold in the earth for concealment as bullets whined off nearby rocks. Up the steep mountainside he went, followed by the bandits. As he crested the spur and started down the other side, the firing ceased. He kept going down, half running, half falling until he reached the bottom. He expected the gunfire to resume when the bandits topped the spur, but it did not.

They had given up the chase.

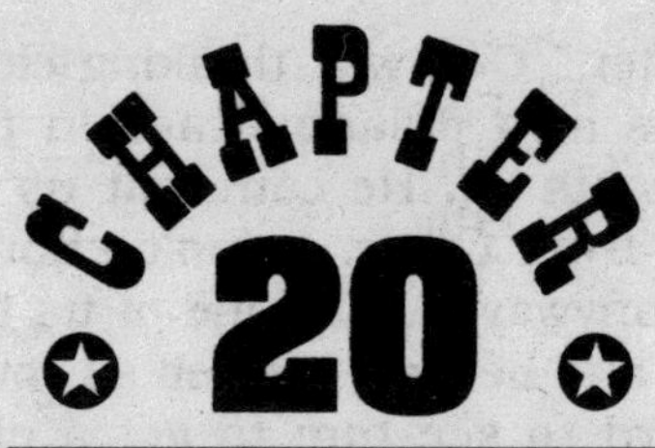

THE WHITE MAN DISAPPEARED OVER THE crest of the spur. The three bandits followed him uphill. They had difficulty running in their high-heeled boots. "Come on," Virge puffed, "let's get that son of a bitch."

Suddenly Gus pulled up, breathing hard. "No," he said. "Let him go."

Virge looked back. "Why? Hell, Gus, he just killed—"

Gus held up a hand. "What if he ain't alone? What if there's more of 'em—whoever they are—up in these mountains? He could be leading us into an ambush."

"And what if he *is* alone?" Virge said. "Are

you just going to let him get away with what he done to Bill?"

"No matter." Gus was thinking clearly now. "He's got us at a disadvantage in there. It's where he wants us. He can split us up there, pick us off from cover. I don't know as we'd catch him, anyway. Ain't none of us that quick on our feet, and he's got himself so covered with dirt it's hard to see him to get a clean shot unless you're right on top of him."

Virge shook his head. "I don't like it."

Gus had another idea. "We got something he wants—water. I don't care who he is, sooner or later he's got to come to the spring."

"That's right," said Virge, brightening. "We can cover the spring from the ranch house with our rifles."

Paco soured that idea. "Not after dark," he pointed out. "What is to stop this man from coming to the spring then, when we cannot see him?"

"So much the better," Virge said. "We'll go down there and set an ambush for him."

Gus bit his lower lip. "No, Paco's right. Whoever this hombre is, he's sneaky as an Injun—sneakier. Christ knows how he surprised Bill in that damn open field—and Bill was half-Injun himself. If we leave cover and go down to the spring after dark, we could be playing right into his hands."

"So what *do* we do?" Virge wanted to know.

"We wait for our horses to come back tomorrow, then we catch them, mount up, and get the hell out of here."

"And what if this fella or his friends has got our horses tied up somewhere?"

"We'll worry about that if it happens. Come on, let's get back to the camp. I don't like leaving that woman alone for too long."

Gus and Virge turned back down the mountain, but Paco was still looking toward the crest. "I do not understand," he said. "Who *is* that man? And what does he want with us?"

"I don't know," Gus said, "and frankly I don't care. He's here, and that's enough for me. Come on, it'll be dark soon."

In the cover of some rocks Sam paused and looked back. He eased his tender ankle and swore softly. Grissom and his men were not coming after him. If he could have drawn them deeper into these mountains, he might have done them some damage, especially if he could have kept them out here after dark.

Cautiously he scouted his back trail, making a long circle around it in case the bandits were trying to trick him. When he crested the spur again, he saw the bandits returning to the ruined ranch house. It was the first time he had gotten a good look at them. There was a tall, rangy one built much like Sam himself—that must be Grissom; a shorter fellow wearing the sombrero and burnt-orange jacket of a vaquero;

and a skinny blond who rolled his hips as he walked—the typical fast gun.

Sam had hung on to his undershirt—both to protect himself from the sun and because he might have use for it later. He put it back on and returned to where he'd left Carolyn, on the far side of the mountain spur. The western sky was a streak of mauve with a band of gold beneath it, caused by the setting sun. Carolyn rose from her hiding place as Sam approached. She looked worried.

"I heard gunfire. Are you all right?"

"Yeah," Sam said.

She hugged him with relief. Sam smiled at her unusual display of emotion, then he said, "I killed one of the gang and ran off their horses."

"You killed one? Without a gun?"

"Yeah." Sam did not elaborate. "A big fellow, called Bill, looked like a breed."

Carolyn's pale forehead creased in a frown. "Cherokee Bill. He's a dangerous man."

"Not anymore," Sam said. "The rest of them chased me into the mountains, but they didn't come any further."

Carolyn stepped back. "I'm dying of thirst. At least with the sun going down, it's not as hot."

"Getting water is our next step. I was hoping to sneak into Grissom's camp and free that woman, but they'll be on their guard now. They'll probably be awake all night. We need to keep them from their horses. It's likely the horses'll come back to the spring tonight for water, then graze nearby tomorrow."

"How are you going to keep Grissom away from them? We don't have any rope to catch them and tie them up with."

"Maybe I can run them off again," Sam said. "If I just had a rifle—a pistol, even."

Sam found a spot among the rocks and lay down. Carolyn had kept his hat. Now he put it on and tilted it over his eyes.

"What are you doing?" Carolyn asked.

"Taking a nap. It might be the last chance we get for a while. You'd be advised to do the same."

Carolyn hesitated, then she found a spot and lay down, too.

It was night. Crickets chirped a raucous symphony around the old ranch house. The three bandits leaned against the crumbling adobe wall, staring into the darkness, fingers curled around the trigger guards of their rifles. Below them the spring was made visible by the faint reflection of moonlight off its surface. Paco was scared; Gus was cool and determined. Virge looked over his shoulder, to where Beth McNally sat against the wall nearby. She was as much on edge as they were, waiting—hoping—for something to happen.

"Keep your mind on what you're doing," Gus whispered, nudging Virge. "Time enough for her later." Gus had conceded the woman to Virge for now. He would deal with the ex-cowboy later, when they were safely away from here.

From the spring came noises. The outlaws stiffened.

"What was that?" Virge hissed.

The noises continued; they seemed to be coming from more than one spot around the spring. They were faint, as if someone—or something—was moving.

"It is the cattle," said Paco at last, relaxing.

"Cattle?" said Virge.

"Sí. When this rancho was abandoned, the cattle must have gone back to the wild. They hide in the mountain thickets by day, then come to the spring at night, for the water."

As if to confirm what Paco had said, a loud bellow split the darkness, followed by another. Virge looked relieved. He'd heard the sound of bulls too many times in Texas not to know what they were.

There was another noise, just behind them. The three men whirled, guns ready to fire—but it was only Beth McNally, stretching out. She saw their frightened reaction, and she laughed at them, a mad laugh.

"I hope he kills you all," she told them.

Gus stepped over and backhanded her across the mouth. "That ain't likely," he said.

Down by the spring the night was alive with noises, made by cattle and other animals like foxes and javelinas. There was the scurry of rodents and the flapping wings of the owls that hunted them.

Sam lay behind a brushy hillock near a point of the spring opposite the ranch house, waiting for the moon to go down. He had circled the spring to see if the bandits had prepared an ambush for him, but he had found no sign of them. Too bad—he'd have liked to catch them out here in the dark. They were playing it smart.

At last the moon set. Sam slithered over the hillock and made his way down to the spring, with his and Carolyn's four canteens over his shoulder. He paused again at the bottom of the hill, listening. Then he crawled forward, to where an old cottonwood overhung the water, giving cover. His presence disturbed some nearby cattle, who edged away, lowing softly. Sam waited again, but he heard no one coming.

He filled the canteens, then drank from the spring. When he was done, he crawled back up the hillock. In a crouch he moved off, to a little gully where Carolyn waited. He handed her two of the canteens. She drank deeply, then whispered. "That was good. And now?"

"Now we wait," Sam told her.

DAWN BROKE GRAY AND QUIET. MISTS ROSE off the spring. Cattle grazed here and there in the pass. In the background the mountains were still dark and indistinct. Toward the oak grove wild pigs rooted at Cherokee Bill's body. Their grunting could be heard up at the ruined ranch house, where the three bandits rubbed their bleary eyes. They had been on alert all night, but there had been no sign of the strange white man, nor was there one now.

"Maybe he's gone," said Virge.

"Maybe he just wanted to steal a horse for himself," suggested Paco. "Or maybe he is just a crazy man, living in the desert."

"Maybe," said Gus. He shivered with the dawn chill. "It's light enough now, we can build a fire, make some coffee and breakfast." They hadn't lit a fire during the night because they hadn't wanted to present their unknown adversary with a target.

The bandits were tired. They had planned to set a guard rotation during the night, but they had all been too keyed up to sleep. Behind them, against what remained of the adobe wall, Beth McNally was awake, too. She was not far from Cherokee Bill's gear, and Gus had tied her hands and feet so she wouldn't try for the dead man's gun belt. Right now a tear rolled down her grimy cheeks.

"Disappointed?" Gus asked, squatting before her while Virge built a fire. "Did you think that fella was coming to save you?"

"Save me?" She laughed harshly. "I'm past saving. I just wanted to see you end up like your friend out there, with the animals picking at your bones."

"Damn," said Gus, taken aback by her vehemence. "I think I liked you better when you didn't talk."

"There are our horses," said Paco, looking toward the spring.

"I told you they'd be back," Gus said, joining him.

In the growing light two of the horses were now visible, grazing together near the spring. "Where's the other one?" Gus asked.

Paco squinted. "There. Is that it?" He pointed to a shape on the far side of the pass, near the mountains.

"Yeah, I think it is," Gus said. Then he went on, looking at the heights behind them and to one side: "You know, it occurs to me that our friend—or friends—must not have any guns. Rifles, leastways. If they did, they'd have opened up on us from these mountains by now."

That statement, and its apparent truth, made the bandits feel better as they sat down to another meal of coffee, beans, and tortillas. They ate heartily after their long night's vigil.

Gus released Beth's hands and gave her a plate of food and some coffee. "Better eat good, keep your energy up. There'll be two of us riding double now. You might need to do some walking later on."

"And if I don't eat?" Beth said.

"Ask Virge about that. He's taking care of you now."

Beth looked over at the ex-cowboy, who grinned at her. Reluctantly she ate.

When the meal was done, Gus and Virge took their ropes and Paco got his leather reata, and they went out to catch the horses. They retied Beth and left her at the house. "What if that gringo comes for her?" Paco said.

"That's a chance we got to take," Gus told him.

"Yeah," agreed Virge. "I don't think he's around here no more, anyways."

"Either way," Gus said, "let's get those horses and make tracks. We wasted too much time on this trip as it is. I want to get to Arispe and start sampling them señoritas."

They started off the rise. Gus and Paco had their pistols. Virge's rifle had a sling, and he carried the weapon across his back. The sun was up now. The men's shadows were thrown long. Their eyes moved constantly, alert for danger.

The two horses near the spring belonged to Gus and Virge. The animal on the far side of the pass was Paco's. "Always I have to do the walking," the Mexican grumbled as the little group split up.

Virge, the onetime cowboy, roped his horse easily. Gus's animal would let him approach only so close before it shied away, and it took Gus a few minutes to toss a loop over the animal's head. Paco's horse, a gray gelding, was almost to the mountains on the far side of the pass. It remained in one spot as Paco clumped toward it, still grumbling. Paco did not like to walk. A true vaquero only got off his horse to sleep, relieve himself, and make love.

Paco shook out the loop of his leather reata as he neared the horse. The horse looked up. It tried to move away from Paco, but seemingly couldn't. As Paco drew closer he saw why. The animal's right foreleg was bound by a cord made of torn, earth-colored cloth—it might once have been a shirt—which had been staked to the ground.

Paco stopped; he went cold inside. He looked

around carefully, but he saw nothing except grass, a clump of rabbitbrush, and the horse. He didn't know what to do. Transferring the reata to his left hand, he drew his pistol, cocked it, and moved forward.

Suddenly the clump of rabbitbrush exploded from the ground, becoming a bare-chested white man with a knife. Before Paco could swing his pistol to fire, the white man ran full tilt into him, driving the knife deep into his heart. Paco's gun went off as he went down, the bullet smashing the gray gelding's left knee.

Paco fell on his back, legs twitching as the life drained out of him. There were yells from near the spring, where Gus and Virge had seen what happened. As Virge unslung his rifle Sam took the pistol from Paco's hand, unbuckled Paco's shell belt, and put it on. Virge fired the rifle. The bullet buzzed past Sam's head as he pulled his knife from the dead man's chest and stuck it back in his belt. Sam turned and hurried back into the mountains while Virge dropped his horse's rope and began running after him.

"This time I ain't letting you get away!" Virge yelled, sending another shot after the mysterious white man.

"Virge!" shouted Gus. "Come back! Virge! Dammit, you stupid . . . !"

His words were lost as the ex-cowboy chased Paco's killer, dust spurting from beneath his boots. Gus grabbed the lead rope of Virge's horse before the animal could run away again. "Virge!" he cried. He looked back toward the rise, but there was no activity there. If their attacker had friends, they were staying put. He looked after Virge, who was already far distant. He couldn't catch up, not leading the horses, so he stayed put, cursing his partner's impetuousness.

Virge ran past Paco's body, past the crippled horse, following the unknown white man into the mountains. On this side of the pass the mountainside was a jumble of rocks and gullies, and Virge saw his quarry disappear around a fissured boulder.

Virge followed the man, finger on the trigger of his rifle. As he rounded the boulder he expected to see the man fleeing up the hillside before him, but all he saw was more rocks. He didn't understand how the man could have disappeared in the space of a few seconds. He bent down and examined the man's tracks—moccasin tracks. They seemed to head up the hill. Virge started forward, warily, ready to shoot.

"Looking for something?" said a voice from behind him.

Virge whirled, but before he could fire, Sam put two pistol bullets into his groin.

Virge dropped the rifle. He slumped to his knees, clutching his groin. Through his tears he saw a bare-chested white man, covered with dirt, with a clump of rabbitbrush in the Apache-style headband holding back his hair. The man's nose was crooked, and across his cheek was a terrible scar.

"You shot off my balls!" Virge cried.

"That's right," replied Sam. "When I was a boy, I was taught that the offending part of a person's body should be punished. If I sassed my elders, I got my mouth slapped. If I hit my cousin, I got my fingers cracked." He paused. "I saw what you did to that woman."

Virge groaned with pain and fell over. Sam stepped forward, picking up Virge's rifle. Virge rolled around in agony, blood covering his wounded groin. Sam held him still and went through his pockets for spare shells.

"What are you going to do to me now?" Virge said.

"Nothing," said Sam.

"Nothing? But it could take me days to die out here, with a wound like this."

"That's the general idea," Sam told him.

"No," cried Virge. "Please, kill me. Don't leave me to die like this."

Sam turned away, leaving the ex-cowboy to his fate. "Please!" Virge cried, but Sam put the man's words from his mind. As he moved back through the rocks he took the rabbitbrush from his headband and threw it away. Carolyn Manning stepped from her hiding place, shaken by what she had just watched. Sam handed her Virge's rifle and shells, and the two of them headed into the pass.

Near the spring Gus had heard the two pistol shots. They had a finality that he did not like. He looked back at the rise and decided the hell with the woman. He had to get out. With his pistol he shot Virge's horse in the head to prevent their unknown assailant from using it to pursue him. Then he grabbed his own horse's mane, curling the length of rope in his free hand. He swung aboard bareback and galloped away, toward Arispe.

Across the pass Sam saw what Gus had done. He swore, wishing he hadn't given the rifle to Carolyn, and he turned urgently. "Give it to . . ."

But Carolyn had already drawn a bead on the fleeing rider. She fired.

A heartbeat passed, then Gus toppled from the horse.

"Nice shot," Sam commented.

"Believe me, it was my pleasure," Carolyn said.

Opposite them Gus staggered to his feet, holding his left shoulder. He started back for the rise.

"He's still alive," said Sam. "Come on."

Sam ran after the wounded Grissom as Carolyn opened fire with the rifle. Gus headed for the rise, zigzagging to throw off Carolyn's aim. Sam ran as fast as he could, moccasined feet making long strides across the plain, but Gus was too close to the rise for him to catch.

Gus moved up the rise, still holding his

shoulder. Carolyn stopped firing and angled across the plain to the mountain spur. Gus saw her from the corner of his eye, but he was concentrating on escaping from Sam and she appeared only as a blur.

Gus reached the ruined house and dived over the wall. He drew his pistol and snapped off a shot, driving the pursuing Sam to earth. Gus scrambled to his bedroll and got his rifle from its scabbard along with the shells in his saddlebag.

"Trouble?" Beth McNally inquired blandly.

"Shut up, bitch."

Gus hurried back, firing the rifle in Sam's direction, then taking cover behind the crumbling wall. The rifle slug was in his upper arm. The blood flowed freely when he took his hand pressure off, but there was no pain yet. That would come later. The wound was not fatal, and he could still use the arm a bit. He'd seen men fight with a lot worse.

A bullet from the mountain spur chipped the adobe by Gus's face, making him duck. Gus swore. He had suspected all along that there was more than one enemy out there. It was only a matter of time before whoever was on that spur got above him, and when that happened, he would be a sitting duck. He had no horse now, and if he tried to break out, the fellow who'd been chasing him would have a clean shot. Plus he was cut off from water. He was finished—or was he?

Sam had taken cover in a fold of earth partway down the rise. Above him Grissom called out, "Tell me something, mister. Who are you, anyway?"

"The name's Sam Slater."

There was a sharp intake of breath. "The bounty hunter? The one they call the Regulator?"

"That's right."

"What do you want with me?"

"Business, Grissom. Business."

"Well, I'm flattered that somebody with your reputation should come after me, Slater. I truly am. But you made yourself one miscalculation."

"What's that?" Sam cried.

Gus crawled back and cut the rope that bound Beth's ankles. He grabbed her arm and yanked her to her feet. He shoved her forward, pushing her through what had once been the doorway of the house. He held her in front of him as a shield and put the pistol to her head. "You forgot about this woman. Give up, Slater, you and your friend, or I'll kill her."

Sam said nothing. Up the mountain he saw Carolyn raise the rifle, and he motioned her not to shoot. There was too much chance of hitting the captive woman. Carolyn did not like the order, but she held her fire.

"I mean it!" yelled Grissom. "It won't be a slow death, either." He lowered the pistol and shot Beth McNally in the foot. Beth cried out. She tried to go down, but Gus held her up.

Sam clenched his fists in rage.

Gus laughed, ignoring the pain of his own

wound, sweat running down his face. "I can make this last a long time, Slater—near as long as an Apache could. How much pain can you watch her take?"

The silence was broken only by Beth's pained whimperings.

"Throw down your guns," Gus ordered, "and come on out. Do it now, or I'll put a bullet in the other foot."

Sam punched the ground and swore. Even if it meant his own life, he couldn't be the cause of this woman's further suffering. He knew what slow death could be like—he'd seen it too many times when he lived among the Apaches.

"You win, Grissom. I'm coming out." Sam stood, tossing away his pistol and raising his hands.

"Your friend, too," Gus cried.

Sam motioned to Carolyn. She didn't want to come out; her rifle remained poised. "We got no choice," Sam told her.

"Now!" said Gus, pointing the pistol at Beth's other foot. Beth bit her lip, trying not to cry, and the resulting sobs sounded all the more pitiful.

Reluctantly Carolyn pitched the rifle in front of her. She stood and moved down the mountainside toward the ranch house.

Gus stared at her in amazement. Then, to Sam's surprise, he burst out laughing. "Carrie? What the hell are you doing here?"

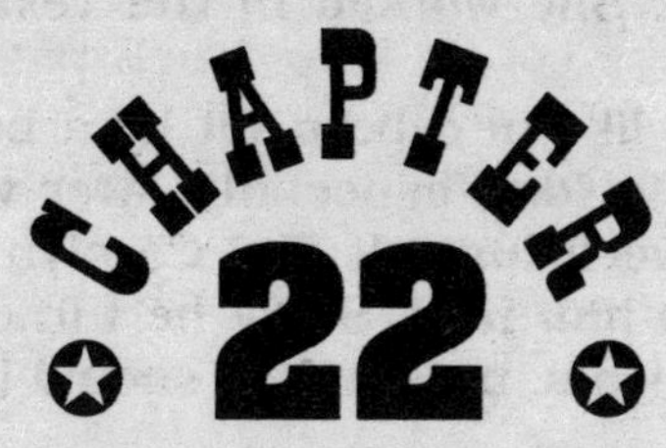

NOW IT WAS SAM'S TURN TO BE AMAZED. "You know her?"

"Know her?" Gus laughed again. "Hell, I lived with her for a year and a half. Didn't she tell you that?"

Sam looked over at Carolyn, but her eyes were fixed on Grissom. Sam said, "She told me you'd killed her father and brother in a bank robbery."

Grissom kept the pistol against Beth McNally's temple. "Well, I reckon she put one over on the great Regulator, didn't she?"

"I reckon she did," Sam said.

Gus went on, enjoying this. "Carrie's a"—he

searched for a polite word—"'fancy lady' from Fort Griffin. She worked in the Texas House there."

Sam felt like he'd been hit by a body blow. He felt like a fool, especially after what had passed between himself and Carolyn. Carolyn was close to him now. Stiffly he turned to her. "My compliments, ma'am. You should have been an actress."

"I considered it," she replied, looking at him. "But the opportunities weren't there, and I needed to feed myself and keep a roof over my head, so I became a whore instead."

"And your accent, all that high-toned speech?"

Carolyn shrugged. "I *am* from New Hampshire. As for the rest, I've had a lot of well-bred customers over the years. I copied their manners, their way of talking. It wasn't hard." Carolyn seemed suddenly transformed. She had become harder somehow, a woman accustomed to life's reverses. The short haircut seemed appropriate for her now, accentuating her high cheekbones.

"Why didn't you tell me the truth?" Sam asked.

"Be serious, Sam. Would you have brought me out here if I had?"

"No," Sam admitted. "I suppose I wouldn't."

Gus broke in. "Which brings me back to my original question, Carrie. Why *are* you here?"

Carolyn's green eyes flashed. "You know

damn well why I'm here, you son of a bitch. I came to pay you back for what you did to me."

Gus let Beth McNally go. She sank to the ground, moaning with pain from the bullet wound in her foot. To Carolyn Gus said, "You went through this hell just for revenge?"

"That's right, you bastard, and I'd have gone through a hundred times worse. I loved you, Gus, and you took advantage of me. I came here to kill you."

Gus looked at the pistol in his hand. "Well, I'm afraid that ain't going to happen. More like the other way around, if anything. Seems you come a long way for nothing."

Sam spoke to Carolyn. "Is this the fellow you talked about, the one that burned you so bad? What did he do, run out on you?"

Carolyn kept her eyes on Gus. "He ran out, all right. Ran out and stole all my money, too. Near three thousand dollars, it was. I'd been saving that money, dollar by dollar, since the day I got started in the game—and believe me, it ain't easy to save when you're in the game. That money was going to get me out of whorehouses and give me a life of my own. Then you stole it, Gus, you son of a—"

She started forward, but Gus leveled the pistol at her and she stopped.

Gus seemed to feel remorse for what he'd done. "Come on, Carrie. Don't go on so. You look good, you know. Seeing you here like this, it makes me think about all the good times we had. It makes me think maybe I made a mistake when I—"

"Oh, don't give me that crap, Gus."

"I mean it, Carrie. It ain't like I wanted to hurt you or nothing. But things was getting hot for me in Texas. I needed money, and I—"

"Oh, no, you didn't hurt me. You destroyed my life, that's all."

"I can make it up to you, Carrie. I took more than thirty-eight thousand from that bank in San Miguel. It's in two grain sacks by my saddle—count it, if you don't believe me. We can split it, you and me. We'll take that and your money and we'll go live like kings. We can open up our own place. Hell, if we invest right, we won't have to work at all. What do you say, Carrie? Forget what happened and come with me."

Carolyn put her hands on her hips. "Do you expect me to fall for that line of horse manure?"

"It's no line, Carrie. I could just kill you, or leave you here. I don't have to share a cent. I'm asking you 'cause I want you to come with me. I miss you." Then he grinned. "Besides, say what you like, the real reason you're here is because you still love me."

Carolyn said nothing. The emotions working across her face said it for her. Sam was still dumbfounded by what had happened, though he didn't know why. He'd learned long ago never to be surprised by anything women did.

Gus continued. "Come on, Carrie. What do you say?"

Carolyn's mask of resolve began to crack.

"Say you'll do it," Gus implored. "It'll be like old times. It'll be better even, 'cause we'll be rich."

Carolyn indicated Sam and Beth McNally. "What about them?"

"I promise, I won't kill them. They're no danger to me now. They can't follow us—there's only one horse left."

Carolyn nodded agreement. Then she smiled at her old lover. "All right, Gus. You win, like always. I'll go with you."

Still holding the pistol on Sam, Gus opened his free arm, the wounded one, to her.

Carolyn hesitated, then crossed to him. They hugged, and she kissed his cheek. As they drew apart she reached in the waistband of her riding skirt and pulled something out. It was the tiny Moore "teat-cartridge" pistol. Gus saw what she had done and his eyes went wide as she began pulling the trigger. She emptied six shots into him, at point blank range. He staggered backward with the impact of the bullets. "Ow! Carrie, don't!" Then the shots stopped.

Gus swayed, shock etched on his face. "Carrie . . ." he began. He reached out for her, then he collapsed on his face in the dirt.

Carolyn looked at the body without pity. "I told you I came here to kill you. You should have believed me."

The gunshots faded, echoing down the pass. Sam was stunned. "You had that gun all along."

"That's right," Carolyn replied. "Like you

said, it's the kind you use to pull out and shoot somebody at close range."

"Why didn't you tell me? It might have helped us out of some tight spots."

"I only planned on using it for one thing," Carolyn said. As she spoke she picked Gus's pistol from the ground by his body, and she pointed it at Sam. "Stay where you are, Sam."

Sam had been moving forward, but now he stopped in his tracks.

Carolyn's voice was steady, like the gun in her hand. "I'm leaving you, Sam. I'm taking that horse and the bank money, and I'm getting out of here."

Sam said nothing. He kept his eyes on the gun barrel, judging whether he could jump her without getting killed. He judged that he couldn't.

Carolyn tried to explain. "I didn't plan it this way. I like you, Sam, I really do. You know that from . . . from the other night. If it wasn't for this bank money, I wouldn't do this. But all my life I've wanted to live well. Suddenly I've got the chance, and I'm not about to let it get away. I'd take you with me, but you'd never let me keep that bank money, would you?"

Sam replied in a low voice. "I couldn't. I'm no do-gooder, and maybe some of that money belongs to big companies that won't miss it, but a lot of it belongs to ordinary people. For a lot of 'em it's all the money they got. Without it they stand to lose their homes and businesses, their life savings. If I let you take it—or if I take some of it with you—it puts me on a level with Gus Grissom. That money isn't mine, and I'd have to try and get it back to its rightful owners, if I could."

Carolyn smiled. "That's what I thought. It's too bad. I'm sorry to leave you like this, Sam. I know it will be rough. But you're part Apache. There's a good chance you'll make it back to San Miguel."

Sam indicated the kidnapped woman. He realized that he did not even know her name. "If it was just me, it would be one thing, but what about her? She's hurt, and it's a long way back to San Miguel. She'll never make it, not on foot. I can't let you do it, Carolyn."

"Under the circumstances I don't think there's much you can do to stop me."

"Carolyn, she'll die. You can't leave her here."

Carolyn was unmoved. "Like Gus always said, 'Life's a bitch.' Now if you'll be so kind as to get the late Mr. Grissom's horse and saddle it for me?"

"And if I don't?" Sam said.

"I'll shoot you. I don't want to, but I will."

She meant it. "And if you try anything funny, I'll start up with her where Gus left off. I know a few tricks of my own."

Grissom's horse had made its way back to the bottom of the rise, with the rope still around its neck. While Sam retrieved the animal

Carolyn went into the old house. Beth McNally half crawled, half hobbled after her. "Mind if I get a drink?" Beth asked, faint with pain from her wounded foot.

"What?" said Carolyn, looking over her shoulder. "No. Go ahead."

Beth rested against Cherokee Bill's saddle, spreading her skirt wide. She took Bill's canteen, wiped the neck with her hand, and drank. Meanwhile Carolyn gathered all of the bandits' guns. She emptied the shells and flung them into the brush, with the weapons thrown after. Then she found the grain sacks with the bank money. She found her own money as well, in Grissom's saddlebags. She saw Beth watching her.

"I'm sorry, honey," said Carolyn. "It's not personal."

"That's what they always say," Beth replied.

Sam brought the horse up the rise. He saddled and bridled it under the cover of Carolyn's pistol. When he was done, Carolyn gave him the grain sacks to tie onto the saddle horn. He secured them, and she flourished the pistol.

"Step back."

Sam did, and Carolyn mounted.

They looked at each other, their eyes meeting. Then Sam said, "Carolyn, don't do this."

"Good-bye, Sam."

Carolyn turned the horse and rode down the rise, away from the house. Sam watched her go, feeling anger, frustration, and betrayal in turn.

"Mr. Slater." It was the wounded woman, inside the house.

Sam went to her, and she pulled back her wide skirt, revealing Cherokee Bill's gun belt and pistol which she had hidden beneath it. She slipped the pistol from its holster. "Here."

Sam took the pistol, and he raced down the rise after Carolyn, cocking it. "Carolyn, stop! Come back! I won't let you go!"

Carolyn halted the horse and turned. She saw the pistol pointed at her. "It's loaded," Sam warned.

Carolyn laughed. "You won't shoot a woman, Sam. You're too much of a gentleman. It's your weakness. So long." She turned away once more, flicking the ends of her reins at the horse's rear.

Sam took a deep breath. His eyes misted, possibly with sweat. Then he pulled the trigger.

Dale Colter is the pseudonym of a full-time writer who lives in Maryland with his family.

HarperPaperbacks *By Mail*

NIGHT STALKERS *by Duncan Long*. TF160, an elite helicopter corps, is sent into the Caribbean to settle a sizzling private war.

NIGHT STALKERS—SHINING PATH *by Duncan Long*. The Night Stalkers help the struggling Peruvian government protect itself from terrorist attacks until America's Vice President is captured by the guerillas and all diplomatic tables are turned.

NIGHT STALKERS—GRIM REAPER *by Duncan Long*. This time TF160 must search the dead-cold Antarctic for a renegade nuclear submarine.

NIGHT STALKERS—DESERT WIND *by Duncan Long*. The hot sands of the Sahara blow red with centuries of blood. Night Stalkers are assigned to transport a prince safely across the terrorist-teeming hell.

TROPHY *by Julian Jay Savarin*. Hand-picked pilots. A futuristic fighter plane. A searing thriller about the ultimate airborne confrontation.

STRIKE FIGHTERS—SUDDEN FURY *by Tom Willard* The Strike Fighters fly on the cutting edge of a desperate global mission—a searing military race to stop a fireball of terror.

STRIKE FIGHTERS—BOLD FORAGER *by Tom Willard*. Sacrette and his Strike Fighters battle for freedom in this heart-pounding, modern-day adventure.

STRIKE FIGHTERS: WAR CHARIOT *by Tom Willard*. Commander Sacrette finds himself deep in a bottomless pit of international death and destruction. Players in the world-wide game of terrorism emerge, using fear, shock and sex as weapons.